THE GRAPHIC NOVEL

William Shakespeare

ORIGINAL TEXT VERSION

Script Adaptation: John McDonald
Pencils: Neill Cameron
Inks: Bambos
Colouring: Jason Cardy & Kat Nicholson
Lettering: Nigel Dobbyn

Editor in Chief: Clive Bryant

Henry V: The Graphic Novel
Original Text Version

William Shakespeare

First UK Edition

Published by: Classical Comics Ltd

All enquiries should be addressed to:
Classical Comics Ltd.
PO Box 7280
Litchborough
Towcester
NN12 9AR, UK
Tel: 0845 812 3000

info@classicalcomics.com
www.classicalcomics.com

ISBN: 978-1-906332-00-6

Printed in the UK
by Hampton Printing (Bristol) Ltd

Contents

Dramatis Personæ

King Henry the Fifth
King of England

Duke Of Gloucester
Brother to the King

Duke Of Bedford
Brother to the King

Duke Of Exeter
Uncle to the King

Duke Of York
Cousin to the King

Earl Of Salisbury

Earl Of Westmoreland

Earl Of Warwick

Archbishop Of
Canterbury

Bishop Of Ely

Earl Of Cambridge
Conspirator

Henry, Lord Scroop
of Masham
Conspirator

Sir Thomas Grey
Conspirator

Sir Thomas Erpingham
*Officer in
King Henry's army*

Captain Gower
*Officer in
King Henry's army*

Captain Fluellen
*Officer in
King Henry's army*

Captain Macmorris
*Officer in
King Henry's army*

Captain Jamy
*Officer in
King Henry's army*

John Bates
*Soldier in
King Henry's army*

Alexander Court
*Soldier in
King Henry's army*

Dramatis Personæ

Michael Williams
Soldier in King Henry's army

Pistol
Soldier in King Henry's army

Nym
Soldier in King Henry's army

Bardolph
Soldier in King Henry's army

Boy
Servant

A Herald

Charles the Sixth
King of France

Lewis
The Dauphin

Duke Of Bourbon
French Duke

Duke Of Burgundy
French Duke

Duke Of Orleans
French Duke

The Constable of France

Lord Rambures
French Lord

Lord Grandpré
French Lord

Montjoy
French Herald

Queen Isabel
Queen of France

Katherine
Daughter to Charles and Isabel

Alice
A lady attending on Katherine

Hostess of a tavern
Formerly Mistress Quickly

Chorus

Synopsis

It's the 15th century and the Archbishop of Canterbury, worried over impending legislation that would effectively rob the Church in England of its power and wealth, convinces Henry V to forego this pursuit in favour of laying claim to France. Armed with a legal technicality, Henry decides to take the throne of France by whatever means necessary. The Dauphin's insulting response (sending an ambassador with a gift of tennis balls) convinces Henry that the French will only respond to war. He gathers his army to invade France, but he must also make certain that he leaves enough troops in England to quell any potential rebellions. This leaves him with a relatively small invasion force.

Henry must deal with one plot before even crossing the Channel. Lords Cambridge, Scroop and Grey are discovered to be conspiring to assassinate Henry (instigated by the French). Henry makes a very public example of all three, arresting them in person and seeing to their execution. The army then lays siege to Harfleur, capturing it after sustaining heavy losses. Henry wants to take his army out of France before the onset of winter, but the French are certain they can teach the young king a humiliating lesson on the field of battle. This stiffens Henry's resolve and he decides that if the French want a decisive battle, they'll get it!

While in camp, Henry disguises himself as a common soldier and mingles with his troops before the battle. He talks candidly with his men and they with him. The men may be a little wary of their king, but their willingness to fight the French army is undaunted. Next day at Agincourt, Henry makes the stirring St. Crispin's Day speech, knowing his army is outnumbered five to one. But, aided by the longbows of his archers, Henry wins the day. The French sue for peace, which Henry grants on his own terms. These terms are spelled out in the Treaty of Troyes – Henry will marry Princess Katherine of France and will be named as heir to the French throne. England and France will thus be united in peace.

Act One
Prologue
O FOR A MUSE OF FIRE, THAT WOULD ASCEND THE BRIGHTEST HEAVEN OF INVENTION!
A KINGDOM FOR A STAGE, PRINCES TO ACT AND MONARCHS TO BEHOLD THE SWELLING SCENE!
THEN SHOULD THE WARLIKE HARRY, LIKE HIMSELF, ASSUME THE PORT OF MARS; AND AT HIS HEELS, LEASH'D IN LIKE HOUNDS, SHOULD FAMINE, SWORD AND FIRE CROUCH FOR EMPLOYMENT.

BUT PARDON, GENTLES ALL, THE FLAT UNRAISED SPIRITS THAT HATH DAR'D ON THIS UNWORTHY SCAFFOLD TO BRING FORTH SO GREAT AN OBJECT: CAN THIS COCKPIT HOLD THE VASTY FIELDS OF FRANCE? OR MAY WE CRAM WITHIN THIS WOODEN O THE VERY CASQUES THAT DID AFFRIGHT THE AIR AT AGINCOURT?
O, PARDON! SINCE A CROOKED FIGURE MAY ATTEST IN LITTLE PLACE A MILLION; AND LET US, CIPHERS TO THIS GREAT ACCOMPT, ON YOUR IMAGINARY FORCES WORK.
SUPPOSE WITHIN THE GIRDLE OF THESE WALLS ARE NOW CONFIN'D TWO MIGHTY MONARCHIES, WHOSE HIGH UPREARED AND ABUTTING FRONTS THE PERILOUS, NARROW OCEAN PARTS ASUNDER.
PIECE OUT OUR IMPERFECTIONS WITH YOUR THOUGHTS; INTO A THOUSAND PARTS DIVIDE ONE MAN, AND MAKE IMAGINARY PUISSANCE;
THINK WHEN WE TALK OF HORSES, THAT YOU SEE THEM PRINTING THEIR PROUD HOOFS I' THE RECEIVING EARTH;
FOR 'TIS YOUR THOUGHTS THAT NOW MUST DECK OUR KINGS, CARRY THEM HERE AND THERE, JUMPING O'ER TIMES, TURNING THE ACCOMPLISHMENT OF MANY YEARS INTO AN HOUR-GLASS: FOR THE WHICH SUPPLY, ADMIT ME CHORUS TO THIS HISTORY;
WHO, PROLOGUE-LIKE YOUR HUMBLE PATIENCE PRAY, GENTLY TO HEAR, KINDLY TO JUDGE, OUR PLAY.

Act One
Scene One
LONDON. AN ANTE-CHAMBER IN THE KING'S PALACE...
SPRING, IN THE YEAR 1415 - THE ARCHBISHOP OF CANTERBURY AND THE BISHOP OF ELY ARE DEEP IN CONVERSATION...
MY LORD, I'LL TELL YOU, THAT SELF BILL IS URG'D, WHICH IN THE ELEVENTH YEAR OF THE LAST KING'S REIGN WAS LIKE, AND HAD INDEED AGAINST US PASS'D, BUT THAT THE SCAMBLING AND UNQUIET TIME DID PUSH IT OUT OF FARTHER QUESTION.
BUT HOW, MY LORD, SHALL WE RESIST IT NOW?

IT MUST BE THOUGHT ON. IF IT PASS AGAINST US, WE LOSE THE BETTER HALF OF OUR POSSESSION;
FOR ALL THE TEMPORAL LANDS, WHICH MEN DEVOUT BY TESTAMENT HAVE GIVEN TO THE CHURCH, WOULD THEY STRIP FROM US;
BEING VALU'D THUS:

AS MUCH AS WOULD MAINTAIN, TO THE KING'S HONOUR, FULL FIFTEEN EARLS AND FIFTEEN HUNDRED KNIGHTS, SIX THOUSAND AND TWO HUNDRED GOOD ESQUIRES;
AND, TO RELIEF OF LAZARS AND WEAK AGE, OF INDIGENT FAINT SOULS PAST CORPORAL TOIL, A HUNDRED ALMSHOUSES RIGHT WELL SUPPLI'D;
AND TO THE COFFERS OF THE KING BESIDE, A THOUSAND POUNDS BY THE YEAR. THUS RUNS THE BILL.

THIS WOULD DRINK DEEP.

'TWOULD DRINK THE CUP AND ALL.

BUT WHAT PREVENTION?

THE KING IS FULL OF GRACE, AND FAIR REGARD.
AND A TRUE LOVER OF THE HOLY CHURCH.
THE COURSES OF HIS YOUTH PROMIS'D IT NOT. THE BREATH NO SOONER LEFT HIS FATHER'S BODY, BUT THAT HIS WILDNESS, MORTIFI'D IN HIM, SEEM'D TO DIE TOO;

YEA, AT THAT VERY MOMENT CONSIDERATION, LIKE AN ANGEL CAME, AND WHIPP'D THE OFFENDING ADAM OUT OF HIM, LEAVING HIS BODY AS A PARADISE, TO ENVELOP AND CONTAIN CELESTIAL SPIRITS.
NEVER WAS SUCH A SUDDEN SCHOLAR MADE; NEVER CAME REFORMATION IN A FLOOD, WITH SUCH A HEADY CURRANCE, SCOURING FAULTS;
NOR NEVER HYDRA-HEADED WILFULNESS SO SOON DID LOSE HIS SEAT, AND ALL AT ONCE, AS IN THIS KING.
WE ARE BLESSED IN THE CHANGE.
HEAR HIM BUT REASON IN DIVINITY, AND, ALL-ADMIRING, WITH AN INWARD WISH YOU WOULD DESIRE THE KING WERE MADE A PRELATE:
HEAR HIM DEBATE OF COMMONWEALTH AFFAIRS, YOU WOULD SAY, IT HATH BEEN ALL-IN-ALL HIS STUDY:
LIST HIS DISCOURSE OF WAR, AND YOU SHALL HEAR A FEARFUL BATTLE RENDER'D YOU IN MUSIC:
TURN HIM TO ANY CAUSE OF POLICY, THE GORDIAN KNOT OF IT HE WILL UNLOOSE, FAMILIAR AS HIS GARTER;

THAT, WHEN HE SPEAKS, THE AIR, A CHARTER'D LIBERTINE, IS STILL, AND THE MUTE WONDER LURKETH IN MEN'S EARS, TO STEAL HIS SWEET AND HONEY'D SENTENCES;
SO THAT THE ART AND PRACTIC PART OF LIFE MUST BE THE MISTRESS TO THIS THEORIC:
WHICH IS A WONDER, HOW HIS GRACE SHOULD GLEAN IT, SINCE HIS ADDICTION WAS TO COURSES VAIN; HIS COMPANIES UNLETTER'D, RUDE AND SHALLOW; HIS HOURS FILL'D UP WITH RIOTS, BANQUETS, SPORTS, AND NEVER NOTED IN HIM ANY STUDY, ANY RETIREMENT, ANY SEQUESTRATION FROM OPEN HAUNTS AND POPULARITY.

THE STRAWBERRY GROWS UNDERNEATH THE NETTLE, AND WHOLESOME BERRIES THRIVE AND RIPEN BEST, NEIGHBOUR'D BY FRUIT OF BASER QUALITY:
AND SO THE PRINCE OBSCUR'D HIS CONTEMPLATION UNDER THE VEIL OF WILDNESS; WHICH, NO DOUBT, GREW LIKE THE SUMMER GRASS, FASTEST BY NIGHT, UNSEEN, YET CRESCIVE IN HIS FACULTY.
IT MUST BE SO; FOR MIRACLES ARE CEAS'D; AND THEREFORE WE MUST NEEDS ADMIT THE MEANS, HOW THINGS ARE PERFECTED.

BUT, MY GOOD LORD, HOW NOW FOR MITIGATION OF THIS BILL URG'D BY THE COMMONS? DOTH HIS MAJESTY INCLINE TO IT, OR NO?
HE SEEMS INDIFFERENT, OR, RATHER, SWAYING MORE UPON OUR PART, THAN CHERISHING THE EXHIBITERS AGAINST US; FOR I HAVE MADE AN OFFER TO HIS MAJESTY, -- UPON OUR SPIRITUAL CONVOCATION AND IN REGARD OF CAUSES NOW IN HAND, WHICH I HAVE OPEN'D TO HIS GRACE AT LARGE, AS TOUCHING FRANCE, -- TO GIVE A GREATER SUM THAN EVER AT ONE TIME THE CLERGY YET DID TO HIS PREDECESSORS PART WITHAL.

HOW DID THIS OFFER SEEM RECEIVED, MY LORD?
WITH GOOD ACCEPTANCE OF HIS MAJESTY; SAVE THAT THERE WAS NOT TIME ENOUGH TO HEAR, AS I PERCEIVED HIS GRACE WOULD FAIN HAVE DONE, THE SEVERALS AND UNHIDDEN PASSAGES OF HIS TRUE TITLES TO SOME CERTAIN DUKEDOMS AND GENERALLY TO THE CROWN AND SEAT OF FRANCE DERIV'D FROM EDWARD, HIS GREAT-GRANDFATHER.

WHAT WAS THE IMPEDIMENT THAT BROKE THIS OFF?
THE FRENCH AMBASSADOR UPON THAT INSTANT CRAV'D AUDIENCE; AND THE HOUR, I THINK, IS COME, TO GIVE HIM HEARING. IS IT FOUR O'CLOCK?
IT IS.

THEN GO WE IN, TO KNOW HIS EMBASSY, WHICH I COULD WITH A READY GUESS DECLARE, BEFORE THE FRENCHMAN SPEAK A WORD OF IT.
I'LL WAIT UPON YOU, AND I LONG TO HEAR IT.

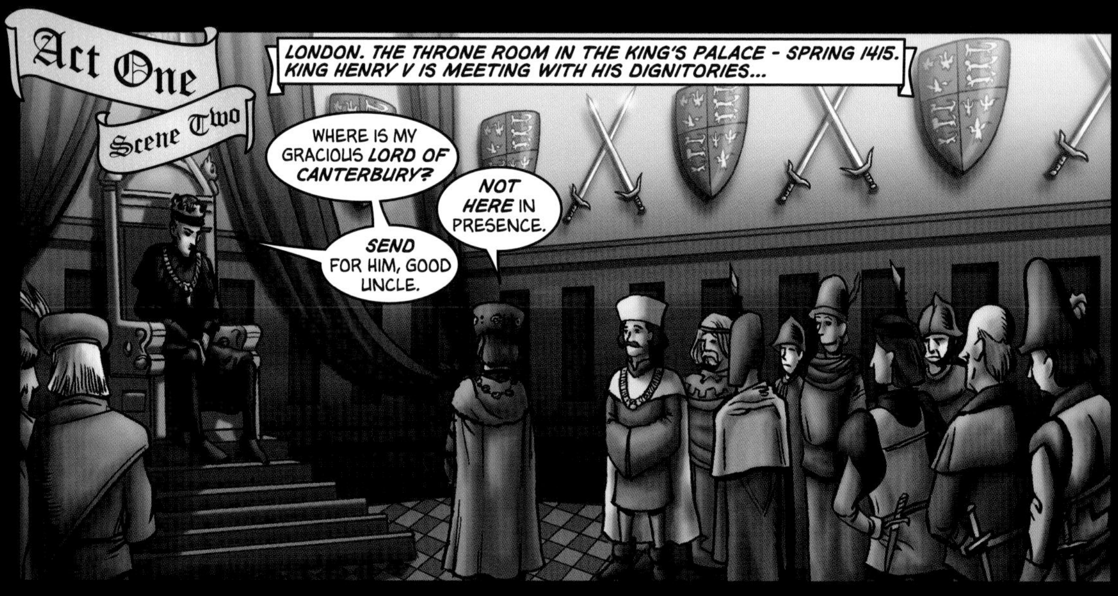
Act One
Scene Two
LONDON. THE THRONE ROOM IN THE KING'S PALACE - SPRING 1415. KING HENRY V IS MEETING WITH HIS DIGNITORIES...
WHERE IS MY GRACIOUS LORD OF CANTERBURY?
NOT HERE IN PRESENCE.
SEND FOR HIM, GOOD UNCLE.

SHALL WE CALL IN THE AMBASSADOR, MY LIEGE?
NOT YET, MY COUSIN: WE WOULD BE RESOLV'D, BEFORE WE HEAR HIM, OF SOME THINGS OF WEIGHT THAT TASK OUR THOUGHTS, CONCERNING US AND FRANCE.
GOD AND HIS ANGELS GUARD YOUR SACRED THRONE AND MAKE YOU LONG BECOME IT!
SURE, WE THANK YOU.
MY LEARNED LORD, WE PRAY YOU TO PROCEED, AND JUSTLY AND RELIGIOUSLY UNFOLD, WHY THE LAW SALIQUE THAT THEY HAVE IN FRANCE, OR SHOULD, OR SHOULD NOT, BAR US IN OUR CLAIM.

AND GOD FORBID, MY DEAR AND FAITHFUL LORD, THAT YOU SHOULD FASHION, WREST, OR BOW YOUR READING, OR NICELY CHARGE YOUR UNDERSTANDING SOUL. WITH OPENING TITLES MISCREATE, WHOSE RIGHT SUITS NOT IN NATIVE COLOURS WITH THE TRUTH;
FOR GOD DOTH KNOW, HOW MANY, NOW IN HEALTH, SHALL DROP THEIR BLOOD IN APPROBATION OF WHAT YOUR REVERENCE SHALL INCITE US TO. THEREFORE TAKE HEED HOW YOU IMPAWN OUR PERSON, HOW YOU AWAKE OUR SLEEPING SWORD OF WAR:
WE CHARGE YOU, IN THE NAME OF GOD, TAKE HEED;
FOR NEVER TWO SUCH KINGDOMS DID CONTEND WITHOUT MUCH FALL OF BLOOD; WHOSE GUILTLESS DROPS ARE EVERY ONE A WOE, A SORE COMPLAINT 'GAINST HIM WHOSE WRONGS GIVE EDGE UNTO THE SWORDS THAT MAKE SUCH WASTE IN BRIEF MORTALITY.
UNDER THIS CONJURATION, SPEAK, MY LORD, AND WE WILL HEAR, NOTE, AND BELIEVE IN HEART, THAT WHAT YOU SPEAK IS IN YOUR CONSCIENCE WASH'D, AS PURE AS SIN WITH BAPTISM.

THEN HEAR ME, GRACIOUS SOVEREIGN, AND YOU PEERS, THAT OWE YOURSELVES, YOUR LIVES, AND SERVICES, TO THIS IMPERIAL THRONE. -- THERE IS NO BAR TO MAKE AGAINST YOUR HIGHNESS' CLAIM TO FRANCE. BUT THIS, WHICH THEY PRODUCE FROM PHARAMOND, --
"IN TERRAM SALICAM MULIERES NE SUCCEDANT," "NO WOMAN SHALL SUCCEED IN SALIQUE LAND:" WHICH SALIQUE LAND THE FRENCH UNJUSTLY GLOZE TO BE THE REALM OF FRANCE, AND PHARAMOND THE FOUNDER OF THIS LAW, AND FEMALE BAR.
YET THEIR OWN AUTHORS FAITHFULLY AFFIRM, THAT THE LAND SALIQUE IS IN GERMANY, BETWEEN THE FLOODS OF SALA AND OF ELBE;

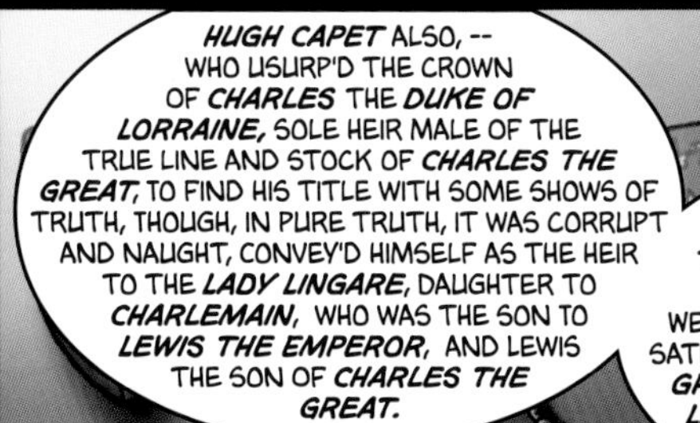
WHERE CHARLES THE GREAT, HAVING SUBDU'D THE SAXONS, THERE LEFT BEHIND AND SETTLED CERTAIN FRENCH; WHO, HOLDING IN DISDAIN THE GERMAN WOMEN, FOR SOME DISHONEST MANNERS OF THEIR LIFE, ESTABLISH'D THEN THIS LAW, -- TO WIT, NO FEMALE SHOULD BE INHERITRIX IN SALIQUE LAND:
WHICH SALIQUE, AS I SAID, 'TWIXT ELBE AND SALA, IS AT THIS DAY IN GERMANY CALL'D MEISEN. THEN DOTH IT WELL APPEAR THE SALIQUE LAW WAS NOT DEVISED FOR THE REALM OF FRANCE;
NOR DID THE FRENCH POSSESS THE SALIQUE LAND UNTIL FOUR HUNDRED ONE-AND-TWENTY YEARS AFTER DEFUNCTION OF KING PHARAMOND, IDLY SUPPOS'D THE FOUNDER OF THIS LAW;

WHO DIED WITHIN THE YEAR OF OUR REDEMPTION FOUR HUNDRED TWENTY-SIX; AND CHARLES THE GREAT SUBDU'D THE SAXONS, AND DID SEAT THE FRENCH BEYOND THE RIVER SALA, IN THE YEAR EIGHT HUNDRED FIVE. BESIDES, THEIR WRITERS SAY, KING PEPIN, WHICH DEPOSED CHILDERIC, DID, AS HEIR GENERAL, BEING DESCENDED OF BLITHILD, WHICH WAS DAUGHTER TO KING CLOTHAIR, MAKE CLAIM AND TITLE TO THE CROWN OF FRANCE.

HUGH CAPET ALSO, -- WHO USURP'D THE CROWN OF CHARLES THE DUKE OF LORRAINE, SOLE HEIR MALE OF THE TRUE LINE AND STOCK OF CHARLES THE GREAT, TO FIND HIS TITLE WITH SOME SHOWS OF TRUTH, THOUGH, IN PURE TRUTH, IT WAS CORRUPT AND NAUGHT, CONVEY'D HIMSELF AS THE HEIR TO THE LADY LINGARE, DAUGHTER TO CHARLEMAIN, WHO WAS THE SON TO LEWIS THE EMPEROR, AND LEWIS THE SON OF CHARLES THE GREAT.
ALSO, KING LEWIS THE TENTH, WHO WAS SOLE HEIR TO THE USURPER CAPET, COULD NOT KEEP QUIET IN HIS CONSCIENCE, WEARING THE CROWN OF FRANCE, TILL SATISFIED THAT FAIR QUEEN ISABEL, HIS GRANDMOTHER, WAS LINEAL OF THE LADY ERMENGARE, DAUGHTER TO CHARLES, THE FORESAID DUKE OF LORRAINE;
BY THE WHICH MARRIAGE THE LINE OF CHARLES THE GREAT WAS RE-UNITED TO THE CROWN OF FRANCE. SO THAT, AS CLEAR AS IS THE SUMMER'S SUN, KING PEPIN'S TITLE AND HUGH CAPET'S CLAIM, KING LEWIS HIS SATISFACTION, ALL APPEAR TO HOLD IN RIGHT AND TITLE OF THE FEMALE. SO DO THE KINGS OF FRANCE UNTO THIS DAY; HOWBEIT THEY WOULD HOLD UP THIS SALIQUE LAW, TO BAR YOUR HIGHNESS CLAIMING FROM THE FEMALE; AND RATHER CHOOSE TO HIDE THEM IN A NET, THAN AMPLY TO IMBAR THEIR CROOKED TITLES USURP'D FROM YOU AND YOUR PROGENITORS.

MAY I WITH RIGHT AND CONSCIENCE MAKE THIS CLAIM?
THE SIN UPON MY HEAD, DREAD SOVEREIGN! FOR IN THE BOOK OF NUMBERS IS IT WRIT, WHEN THE MAN DIES, LET THE INHERITANCE DESCEND UNTO THE DAUGHTER.
GRACIOUS LORD, STAND FOR YOUR OWN! UNWIND YOUR BLOODY FLAG! LOOK BACK INTO YOUR MIGHTY ANCESTORS!

GO, MY DREAD LORD, TO YOUR GREAT-GRANDSIRE'S TOMB, FROM WHOM YOU CLAIM: INVOKE HIS WARLIKE SPIRIT, AND YOUR GREAT-UNCLE'S, EDWARD THE BLACK PRINCE, WHO ON THE FRENCH GROUND PLAY'D A TRAGEDY, MAKING DEFEAT ON THE FULL POWER OF FRANCE, WHILES HIS MOST MIGHTY FATHER ON A HILL STOOD SMILING TO BEHOLD HIS LION'S WHELP FORAGE IN BLOOD OF FRENCH NOBILITY.

O NOBLE ENGLISH! THAT COULD ENTERTAIN WITH HALF THEIR FORCES THE FULL PRIDE OF FRANCE, AND LET ANOTHER HALF STAND LAUGHING BY, ALL OUT OF WORK AND COLD FOR ACTION.
AWAKE REMEMBRANCE OF THESE VALIANT DEAD, AND WITH YOUR PUISSANT ARM RENEW THEIR FEATS. YOU ARE THEIR HEIR; YOU SIT UPON THEIR THRONE; THE BLOOD AND COURAGE THAT RENOWNED THEM RUNS IN YOUR VEINS; AND MY THRICE-PUISSANT LIEGE IS IN THE VERY MAY-MORN OF HIS YOUTH, RIPE FOR EXPLOITS AND MIGHTY ENTERPRISES.
YOUR BROTHER KINGS AND MONARCHS OF THE EARTH DO ALL EXPECT THAT YOU SHOULD ROUSE YOURSELF, AS DID THE FORMER LIONS OF YOUR BLOOD.
THEY KNOW YOUR GRACE HATH CAUSE, AND MEANS, AND MIGHT: -- SO HATH YOUR HIGHNESS -- NEVER KING OF ENGLAND HAD NOBLES RICHER, AND MORE LOYAL SUBJECTS, WHOSE HEARTS HAVE LEFT THEIR BODIES HERE IN ENGLAND, AND LIE PAVILION'D IN THE FIELDS OF FRANCE.

O, LET THEIR BODIES FOLLOW, MY DEAR LIEGE, WITH BLOOD, AND SWORD, AND FIRE; TO WIN YOUR RIGHT: IN AID WHEREOF, WE OF THE SPIRITUALTY WILL RAISE YOUR HIGHNESS SUCH A MIGHTY SUM, AS NEVER DID THE CLERGY AT ONE TIME BRING IN TO ANY OF YOUR ANCESTORS.
WE MUST NOT ONLY ARM TO INVADE THE FRENCH, BUT LAY DOWN OUR PROPORTIONS TO DEFEND AGAINST THE SCOT, WHO WILL MAKE ROAD UPON US WITH ALL ADVANTAGES.
THEY OF THOSE MARCHES, GRACIOUS SOVEREIGN, SHALL BE A WALL SUFFICIENT TO DEFEND OUR INLAND FROM THE PILFERING BORDERERS.
WE DO NOT MEAN THE COURSING SNATCHERS ONLY, BUT FEAR THE MAIN INTENDMENT OF THE SCOT, WHO HATH BEEN STILL A GIDDY NEIGHBOUR TO US; FOR YOU SHALL READ, THAT MY GREAT-GRANDFATHER NEVER WENT WITH HIS FORCES INTO FRANCE, BUT THAT THE SCOT ON HIS UNFURNISH'D KINGDOM CAME POURING, LIKE THE TIDE INTO A BREACH, WITH AMPLE AND BRIM FULLNESS OF HIS FORCE, GALLING THE GLEANED LAND WITH HOT ASSAYS, GIRDING WITH GRIEVOUS SIEGE CASTLES AND TOWNS;
THAT ENGLAND, BEING EMPTY OF DEFENCE, HATH SHOOK AND TREMBLED AT THE ILL NEIGHBOURHOOD.
SHE HATH BEEN THEN MORE FEAR'D THAN HARM'D, MY LIEGE;
FOR HEAR HER BUT EXAMPL'D BY HERSELF: WHEN ALL HER CHIVALRY HATH BEEN IN FRANCE, AND SHE A MOURNING WIDOW OF HER NOBLES, SHE HATH HERSELF NOT ONLY WELL DEFENDED, BUT TAKEN, AND IMPOUNDED AS A STRAY, THE KING OF SCOTS; WHOM SHE DID SEND TO FRANCE, TO FILL KING EDWARD'S FAME WITH PRISONER KINGS, AND MAKE HER CHRONICLE AS RICH WITH PRAISE, AS IS THE OOZE AND BOTTOM OF THE SEA WITH SUNKEN WRECK AND SUMLESS TREASURIES.
BUT THERE'S A SAYING, VERY OLD AND TRUE, "IF THAT YOU WILL FRANCE WIN, THEN WITH SCOTLAND FIRST BEGIN:"
FOR ONCE THE EAGLE ENGLAND BEING IN PREY, TO HER UNGUARDED NEST THE WEASEL SCOT COMES SNEAKING AND SO SUCKS HER PRINCELY EGGS; PLAYING THE MOUSE IN ABSENCE OF THE CAT, TO TEAR AND HAVOC MORE THAN SHE CAN EAT.
IT FOLLOWS THEN, THE CAT MUST STAY AT HOME: YET THAT IS BUT A CRUSH'D NECESSITY; SINCE WE HAVE LOCKS TO SAFEGUARD NECESSARIES, AND PRETTY TRAPS TO CATCH THE PETTY THIEVES.
WHILE THAT THE ARMED HAND DOTH FIGHT ABROAD, THE ADVISED HEAD DEFENDS ITSELF AT HOME: FOR GOVERNMENT, THOUGH HIGH, AND LOW, AND LOWER, PUT INTO PARTS, DOTH KEEP IN ONE CONSENT, CONGREEING IN A FULL AND NATURAL CLOSE, LIKE MUSIC.

THEREFORE DOTH HEAVEN DIVIDE THE STATE OF MAN IN DIVERS FUNCTIONS, SETTING ENDEAVOUR IN CONTINUAL MOTION; TO WHICH IS FIXED, AS AN AIM OR BUTT, OBEDIENCE: FOR SO WORK THE HONEY-BEES, CREATURES, THAT BY A RULE IN NATURE TEACH THE ACT OF ORDER TO A PEOPLED KINGDOM:
THEY HAVE A KING, AND OFFICERS OF SORTS; WHERE SOME, LIKE MAGISTRATES, CORRECT AT HOME, OTHERS, LIKE MERCHANTS, VENTURE TRADE ABROAD, OTHERS, LIKE SOLDIERS, ARMED IN THEIR STINGS, MAKE BOOT UPON THE SUMMER'S VELVET BUDS;

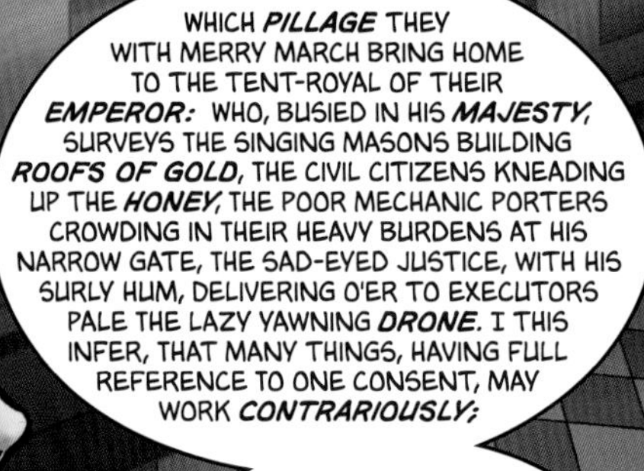

WHICH PILLAGE THEY WITH MERRY MARCH BRING HOME TO THE TENT-ROYAL OF THEIR EMPEROR: WHO, BUSIED IN HIS MAJESTY, SURVEYS THE SINGING MASONS BUILDING ROOFS OF GOLD, THE CIVIL CITIZENS KNEADING UP THE HONEY, THE POOR MECHANIC PORTERS CROWDING IN THEIR HEAVY BURDENS AT HIS NARROW GATE, THE SAD-EYED JUSTICE, WITH HIS SURLY HUM, DELIVERING O'ER TO EXECUTORS PALE THE LAZY YAWNING DRONE. I THIS INFER, THAT MANY THINGS, HAVING FULL REFERENCE TO ONE CONSENT, MAY WORK CONTRARIOUSLY;
AS MANY ARROWS, LOOSED SEVERAL WAYS, COME TO ONE MARK; AS MANY WAYS MEET IN ONE TOWN; AS MANY FRESH STREAMS MEET IN ONE SALT SEA; AS MANY LINES CLOSE IN THE DIAL'S CENTRE; SO MAY A THOUSAND ACTIONS, ONCE AFOOT, END IN ONE PURPOSE, AND BE ALL WELL BORNE WITHOUT DEFEAT.

THEREFORE TO FRANCE, MY LIEGE!
DIVIDE YOUR HAPPY ENGLAND INTO FOUR, WHEREOF TAKE YOU ONE QUARTER INTO FRANCE, AND YOU WITHAL SHALL MAKE ALL GALLIA SHAKE. IF WE, WITH THRICE SUCH POWERS LEFT AT HOME, CANNOT DEFEND OUR OWN DOORS FROM THE DOG, LET US BE WORRIED AND OUR NATION LOSE THE NAME OF HARDINESS AND POLICY.

CALL IN THE MESSENGERS SENT FROM THE DAUPHIN.
NOW ARE WE WELL RESOLV'D: AND, BY GOD'S HELP, AND YOURS, THE NOBLE SINEWS OF OUR POWER, FRANCE BEING OURS, WE'LL BEND IT TO OUR AWE, OR BREAK IT ALL TO PIECES: OR THERE WE'LL SIT, RULING IN LARGE AND AMPLE EMPERY O'ER FRANCE, AND ALL HER ALMOST KINGLY DUKEDOMS, OR LAY THESE BONES IN AN UNWORTHY URN, TOMBLESS, WITH NO REMEMBRANCE OVER THEM:
EITHER OUR HISTORY SHALL WITH FULL MOUTH SPEAK FREELY OF OUR ACTS; OR ELSE OUR GRAVE, LIKE TURKISH MUTE, SHALL HAVE A TONGUELESS MOUTH, NOT WORSHIPP'D WITH A WAXEN EPITAPH.

NOW ARE WE WELL PREPAR'D TO KNOW THE PLEASURE OF OUR FAIR COUSIN DAUPHIN; FOR, WE HEAR, YOUR GREETING IS FROM HIM, NOT FROM THE KING.
MAY'T PLEASE YOUR MAJESTY, TO GIVE US LEAVE FREELY TO RENDER WHAT WE HAVE IN CHARGE;
OR SHALL WE SPARINGLY SHOW YOU FAR OFF THE DAUPHIN'S MEANING, AND OUR EMBASSY?
WE ARE NO TYRANT, BUT A CHRISTIAN KING, UNTO WHOSE GRACE OUR PASSION IS AS SUBJECT, AS ARE OUR WRETCHES FETTER'D IN OUR PRISONS:
THEREFORE, WITH FRANK AND WITH UNCURBED PLAINNESS, TELL US THE DAUPHIN'S MIND.

THUS, THEN, IN FEW.
YOUR HIGHNESS, LATELY SENDING INTO FRANCE, DID CLAIM SOME CERTAIN DUKEDOMS, IN THE RIGHT OF YOUR GREAT PREDECESSOR, KING EDWARD THE THIRD.
IN ANSWER OF WHICH CLAIM, THE PRINCE OUR MASTER SAYS, THAT YOU SAVOUR TOO MUCH OF YOUR YOUTH, AND BIDS YOU BE ADVIS'D THERE'S NOUGHT IN FRANCE THAT CAN BE WITH A NIMBLE GALLIARD WON: YOU CANNOT REVEL INTO DUKEDOMS THERE.
HE THEREFORE SENDS YOU, MEETER FOR YOUR SPIRIT, THIS TUN OF TREASURE; AND, IN LIEU OF THIS, DESIRES YOU, LET THE DUKEDOMS, THAT YOU CLAIM, HEAR NO MORE OF YOU. THIS THE DAUPHIN SPEAKS.
WHAT TREASURE, UNCLE?

TENNIS-BALLS, MY LIEGE.
WE ARE GLAD THE DAUPHIN IS SO PLEASANT WITH US. HIS PRESENT AND YOUR PAINS, WE THANK YOU FOR:
WHEN WE HAVE MATCH'D OUR RACKETS TO THESE BALLS, WE WILL IN FRANCE, BY GOD'S GRACE, PLAY A SET, SHALL STRIKE HIS FATHER'S CROWN INTO THE HAZARD.
TELL HIM, HE HATH MADE A MATCH WITH SUCH A WRANGLER, THAT ALL THE COURTS OF FRANCE WILL BE DISTURB'D WITH CHASES. AND WE UNDERSTAND HIM WELL, HOW HE COMES O'ER US WITH OUR WILDER DAYS, NOT MEASURING WHAT USE WE MADE OF THEM.

WE NEVER VALU'D THIS POOR SEAT OF ENGLAND; AND THEREFORE, LIVING HENCE, DID GIVE OURSELF TO BARBAROUS LICENCE; AS 'TIS EVER COMMON, THAT MEN ARE MERRIEST WHEN THEY ARE FROM HOME. BUT TELL THE DAUPHIN. – I WILL KEEP MY STATE; BE LIKE A KING, AND SHOW MY SAIL OF GREATNESS, WHEN I DO ROUSE ME IN MY THRONE OF FRANCE:
FOR THAT I HAVE LAID BY MY MAJESTY AND PLODDED LIKE A MAN FOR WORKING-DAYS; BUT I WILL RISE THERE WITH SO FULL A GLORY THAT I WILL DAZZLE ALL THE EYES OF FRANCE, YEA, STRIKE THE DAUPHIN BLIND TO LOOK ON US.
AND TELL THE PLEASANT PRINCE, THIS MOCK OF HIS HATH TURN'D HIS BALLS TO GUN-STONES; AND HIS SOUL SHALL STAND SORE CHARGED FOR THE WASTEFUL VENGEANCE THAT SHALL FLY WITH THEM: FOR MANY A THOUSAND WIDOWS SHALL THIS HIS MOCK MOCK OUT OF THEIR DEAR HUSBANDS;

MOCK MOTHERS FROM THEIR SONS, MOCK CASTLES DOWN; AND SOME ARE YET UNGOTTEN AND UNBORN, THAT SHALL HAVE CAUSE TO CURSE THE DAUPHIN'S SCORN.
BUT THIS LIES ALL WITHIN THE WILL OF GOD, TO WHOM I DO APPEAL; AND IN WHOSE NAME, TELL YOU THE DAUPHIN, I AM COMING ON, TO VENGE ME AS I MAY, AND TO PUT FORTH MY RIGHTFUL HAND IN A WELL-HALLOW'D CAUSE.
SO GET YOU HENCE IN PEACE; AND TELL THE DAUPHIN, HIS JEST WILL SAVOUR BUT OF SHALLOW WIT, WHEN THOUSANDS WEEP, MORE THAN DID LAUGH AT IT.

CONVEY THEM WITH SAFE CONDUCT.
FARE YOU WELL.
THIS WAS A MERRY MESSAGE.
WE HOPE TO MAKE THE SENDER BLUSH AT IT. THEREFORE, MY LORDS, OMIT NO HAPPY HOUR, THAT MAY GIVE FURTHERANCE TO OUR EXPEDITION;
FOR WE HAVE NOW NO THOUGHT IN US BUT FRANCE, SAVE THOSE TO GOD, THAT RUN BEFORE OUR BUSINESS.
THEREFORE, LET OUR PROPORTIONS FOR THESE WARS BE SOON COLLECTED, AND ALL THINGS THOUGHT UPON, THAT MAY WITH REASONABLE SWIFTNES ADD MORE FEATHERS TO OUR WINGS; FOR, GOD BEFORE, WE'LL CHIDE THIS DAUPHIN AT HIS FATHER'S DOOR.
THERE-FORE LET EVER MAN NOW TAS HIS THOUGHT, THA THIS FAIR ACTIO MAY ON FOOT BE BROUGHT.

Act Two
Prologue
NOW ALL THE YOUTH OF ENGLAND ARE ON FIRE, AND SILKEN DALLIANCE IN THE WARDROBE LIES: NOW THRIVE THE ARMOURERS, AND HONOUR'S THOUGHT REIGNS SOLELY IN THE BREAST OF EVERY MAN.
THEY SELL THE PASTURE NOW TO BUY THE HORSE; FOLLOWING THE MIRROR OF ALL CHRISTIAN KINGS, WITH WINGED HEELS, AS ENGLISH MERCURIES. FOR NOW SITS EXPECTATION IN THE AIR; AND HIDES A SWORD, FROM HILTS UNTO THE POINT, WITH CROWNS IMPERIAL, CROWNS, AND CORONETS, PROMIS'D TO HARRY AND HIS FOLLOWERS.
THE FRENCH, ADVIS'D BY GOOD INTELLIGENCE OF THIS MOST DREADFUL PREPARATION, SHAKE IN THEIR FEAR, AND WITH PALE POLICY SEEK TO DIVERT THE ENGLISH PURPOSES.

O ENGLAND! MODEL TO THY INWARD GREATNESS, LIKE LITTLE BODY WITH A MIGHTY HEART, WHAT MIGHTST THOU DO, THAT HONOUR WOULD THEE DO, WERE ALL THY CHILDREN KIND AND NATURAL!
BUT SEE THY FAULT!
FRANCE HATH IN THEE FOUND OUT A NEST OF HOLLOW BOSOMS, WHICH HE FILLS WITH TREACHEROUS CROWNS; AND THREE CORRUPTED MEN, ONE, RICHARD EARL OF CAMBRIDGE, AND THE SECOND, HENRY LORD SCROOP OF MASHAM, AND THE THIRD, SIR THOMAS GREY, KNIGHT OF NORTHUMBERLAND, HAVE, FOR THE GILT OF FRANCE, -- O GUILT INDEED! -- CONFIRM'D CONSPIRACY WITH FEARFUL FRANCE;
AND BY THEIR HANDS THIS GRACE OF KINGS MUST DIE, IF HELL AND TREASON HOLD THEIR PROMISES, ERE HE TAKE SHIP FOR FRANCE, AND IN SOUTHAMPTON.
LINGER YOUR PATIENCE ON: AND WE'LL DIGEST THE ABUSE OF DISTANCE; FORCE A PLAY. THE SUM IS PAID; THE TRAITORS ARE AGREED;
THE KING IS SET FROM LONDON; AND THE SCENE IS NOW TRANSPORTED, GENTLES, TO SOUTHAMPTON: THERE IS THE PLAYHOUSE NOW, THERE MUST YOU SIT, AND THENCE TO FRANCE SHALL WE CONVEY YOU SAFE, AND BRING YOU BACK, CHARMING THE NARROW SEAS TO GIVE YOU GENTLE PASS; FOR, IF WE MAY, WE'LL NOT OFFEND ONE STOMACH WITH OUR PLAY. BUT, TILL THE KING COME FORTH, AND NOT TILL THEN, UNTO SOUTHAMPTON DO WE SHIFT OUR SCENE.

Act Two
Scene One
LONDON - THE BOARS HEAD TAVERN, IN EASTCHEAP - SUMMER 1415...
WELL MET, CORPORAL NYM.
GOOD MORROW, LIEUTENANT BARDOLPH.
WHAT, ARE ANCIENT PISTOL AND YOU FRIENDS YET?
FOR MY PART, I CARE NOT: I SAY LITTLE; BUT WHEN TIME SHALL SERVE, THERE SHALL BE SMILES; -- BUT THAT SHALL BE AS IT MAY. I DARE NOT FIGHT; BUT I WILL WINK, AND HOLD OUT MINE IRON. IT IS A SIMPLE ONE; BUT WHAT THOUGH? IT WILL TOAST CHEESE, AND IT WILL ENDURE COLD AS ANOTHER MAN'S SWORD WILL; AND THERE'S AN END.
I WILL BESTOW A BREAKFAST TO MAKE YOU FRIENDS, AND WE'LL BE ALL THREE SWORN BROTHERS TO FRANCE. LET IT BE SO, GOOD CORPORAL NYM.
'FAITH, I WILL LIVE SO LONG AS I MAY, THAT'S THE CERTAIN OF IT; AND WHEN I CANNOT LIVE ANY LONGER, I WILL DO AS I MAY: THAT IS MY REST, THAT IS THE RENDEZVOUS OF IT.
IT IS CERTAIN, CORPORAL, THAT HE IS MARRIED TO NELL QUICKLY; AND, CERTAINLY, SHE DID YOU WRONG, FOR YOU WERE TROTH-PLIGHT TO HER.
I CANNOT TELL; THINGS MUST BE AS THEY MAY: MEN MAY SLEEP, AND THEY MAY HAVE THEIR THROATS ABOUT THEM AT THAT TIME; AND SOME SAY, KNIVES HAVE EDGES. IT MUST BE AS IT MAY: THOUGH PATIENCE BE A TIRED MARE, YET SHE WILL PLOD. THERE MUST BE CONCLUSIONS. WELL, I CANNOT TELL.

HERE COMES ANCIENT PISTOL, AND HIS WIFE. -- GOOD CORPORAL, BE PATIENT HERE.
HOW NOW, MINE HOST PISTOL?
BASE TIKE, CALL'ST THOU ME HOST? NOW, BY THIS HAND I SWEAR, I SCORN THE TERM; NOR SHALL MY NELL KEEP LODGERS.
NO, BY MY TROTH, NOT LONG: FOR WE CANNOT LODGE AND BOARD A DOZEN OR FOURTEEN GENTLEWOMEN, THAT LIVE HONESTLY BY THE PRICK OF THEIR NEEDLES, BUT IT WILL BE THOUGHT WE KEEP A BAWDY-HOUSE STRAIGHT.

O WELL-A-DAY, LADY! IF HE BE NOT DRAWN! NOW WE SHALL SEE WILFUL ADULTERY AND MURDER COMMITTED.

GOOD LIEUTENANT! GOOD CORPORAL! OFFER NOTHING HERE.
PISH!
PISH FOR THEE, ICELAND DOG! THOU PRICK-EAR'D CUR OF ICELAND!

GOOD CORPORAL NYM, SHOW THY VALOUR, AND PUT UP YOUR SWORD.
WILL YOU SHOG OFF?

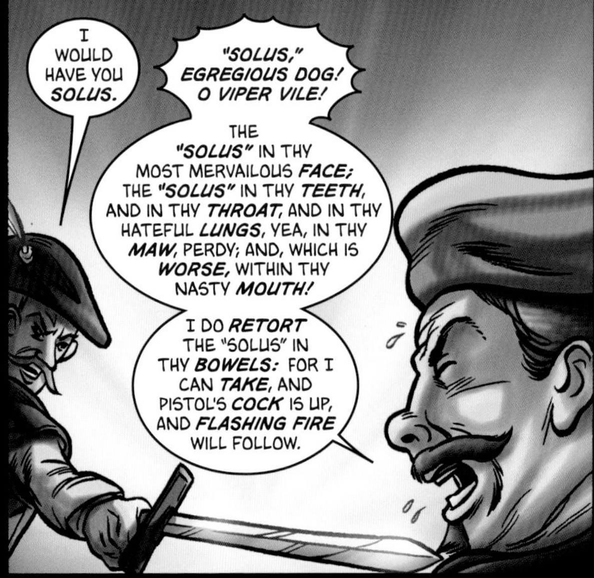
I WOULD HAVE YOU SOLUS.
"SOLUS," EGREGIOUS DOG! O VIPER VILE!
THE "SOLUS" IN THY MOST MERVAILOUS FACE; THE "SOLUS" IN THY TEETH, AND IN THY THROAT, AND IN THY HATEFUL LUNGS, YEA, IN THY MAW, PERDY; AND, WHICH IS WORSE, WITHIN THY NASTY MOUTH!
I DO RETORT THE "SOLUS" IN THY BOWELS: FOR I CAN TAKE, AND PISTOL'S COCK IS UP, AND FLASHING FIRE WILL FOLLOW.

I AM NOT BARBASON; YOU CANNOT CONJURE ME. I HAVE AN HUMOUR TO KNOCK YOU INDIFFERENTLY WELL. IF YOU GROW FOUL WITH ME, PISTOL, I WILL SCOUR YOU WITH MY RAPIER, AS I MAY, IN FAIR TERMS: IF YOU WOULD WALK OFF, I WOULD PRICK YOUR GUTS A LITTLE, IN GOOD TERMS, AS I MAY; AND THAT'S THE HUMOUR OF IT.
O BRAGGART VILE, AND DAMNED FURIOUS WIGHT!
THE GRAVE DOTH GAPE, AND DOTING DEATH IS NEAR; THEREFORE EXHALE.
HEAR ME, HEAR ME WHAT I SAY: -- HE THAT STRIKES THE FIRST STROKE, I'LL RUN HIM UP TO THE HILTS, AS I AM A SOLDIER.
AN OATH OF MICKLE MIGHT, AND FURY SHALL ABATE. GIVE ME THY FIST, THY FORE-FOOT TO ME GIVE; THY SPIRITS ARE MOST TALL.
I WILL CUT THY THROAT, ONE TIME OR OTHER, IN FAIR TERMS: THAT IS THE HUMOUR OF IT.
"COUP LE GORGE!" THAT IS THE WORD. I THEE DEFY AGAIN.
O HOUND OF CRETE, THINK'ST THOU MY SPOUSE TO GET? NO; TO THE SPITAL GO, AND FROM THE POWDERING-TUB OF INFAMY FETCH FORTH THE LAZAR KITE OF CRESSID'S KIND, DOLL TEAR-SHEET SHE BY NAME, AND HER ESPOUSE:
I HAVE, AND I WILL HOLD, THE QUONDAM QUICKLY FOR THE ONLY SHE; AND -- PAUCA, THERE'S ENOUGH.
GO TO.

MINE HOST PISTOL, YOU MUST COME TO MY MASTER, AND YOU, HOSTESS. HE IS VERY SICK, AND WOULD TO BED.
GOOD BARDOLPH, PUT THY FACE BETWEEN HIS SHEETS, AND DO THE OFFICE OF A WARMING-PAN: 'FAITH, HE'S VERY ILL.
AWAY, YOU ROGUE!
BY MY TROTH, HE'LL YIELD THE CROW A PUDDING ONE OF THESE DAYS: THE KING HAS KILL'D HIS HEART. -- GOOD HUSBAND, COME HOME PRESENTLY.

COME, SHALL I MAKE YOU TWO *FRIENDS?* WE MUST TO *FRANCE* TOGETHER. WHY, THE DEVIL, SHOULD WE KEEP *KNIVES* TO CUT ONE ANOTHER'S *THROATS?*
LET *FLOODS* O'ERSWELL, AND FIENDS FOR *FOOD* HOWL ON!
YOU'LL PAY ME THE *EIGHT SHILLINGS* I WON OF YOU AT BETTING?
BASE IS THE SLAVE THAT PAYS.
THAT NOW I WILL HAVE: THAT'S THE *HUMOUR* OF IT.
AS MANHOOD SHALL COMPOUND. *PUSH HOME.*
BY THIS SWORD, HE THAT MAKES THE FIRST THRUST, I'LL *KILL* HIM; *BY THIS SWORD, I WILL.*

SWORD IS AN *OATH*, AND OATHS MUST HAVE THEIR COURSE.
CORPORAL NYM, AN THOU WILT BE *FRIENDS*, BE *FRIENDS*; AN THOU WILT *NOT*, WHY, THEN BE *ENEMIES* WITH *ME* TOO.
PR'YTHEE, *PUT UP.*
I SHALL HAVE MY *EIGHT SHILLINGS* I WON OF YOU AT BETTING?

A NOBLE SHALT THOU HAVE, AND PRESENT PAY; AND LIQUOR LIKEWISE WILL I GIVE TO THEE, AND FRIENDSHIP SHALL COMBINE, AND BROTHERHOOD: I'LL LIVE BY NYM, AND NYM SHALL LIVE BY ME.
IS NOT THIS JUST? FOR I SHALL SUTLER BE UNTO THE CAMP, AND PROFITS WILL ACCRUE.
GIVE ME THY HAND.
I SHALL HAVE MY NOBLE?
IN CASH MOST JUSTLY PAID.
WELL, THEN, THAT'S THE HUMOUR OF'T.
AS EVER YOU COME OF WOMEN, COME IN QUICKLY TO SIR JOHN. AH, POOR HEART! HE IS SO SHAK'D OF A BURNING QUOTIDIAN TERTIAN, THAT IT IS MOST LAMENTABLE TO BEHOLD. SWEET MEN, COME TO HIM.
THE KING HATH RUN BAD HUMOURS ON THE KNIGHT, THAT'S THE EVEN OF IT.
NYM, THOU HAST SPOKE THE RIGHT; HIS HEART IS FRACTED, AND CORROBORATE.
THE KING IS A GOOD KING; BUT IT MUST BE AS IT MAY; HE PASSES SOME HUMOURS, AND CAREERS.
LET US CONDOLE THE KNIGHT; FOR, LAMBKINS, WE WILL LIVE.

Act Two
Scene Two
THE PORT OF SOUTHAMPTON - SUMMER 1415. THE SHIPS ARE PREPARING TO LEAVE FOR FRANCE...
'FORE GOD, HIS GRACE IS BOLD TO TRUST THESE TRAITORS.
THEY SHALL BE APPREHENDED BY-AND-BY.
HOW SMOOTH AND EVEN THEY DO BEAR THEMSELVES! AS IF ALLEGIANCE IN THEIR BOSOMS SAT, CROWNED WITH FAITH, AND CONSTANT LOYALTY.
THE KING HATH NOTE OF ALL THAT THEY INTEND, BY INTERCEPTION WHICH THEY DREAM NOT OF.
NAY, BUT THE MAN THAT WAS HIS BEDFELLOW, WHOM HE HATH DULL'D AND CLOY'D WITH GRACIOUS FAVOURS, THAT HE SHOULD, FOR A FOREIGN PURSE, SO SELL HIS SOVEREIGN'S LIFE TO DEATH AND TREACHERY!

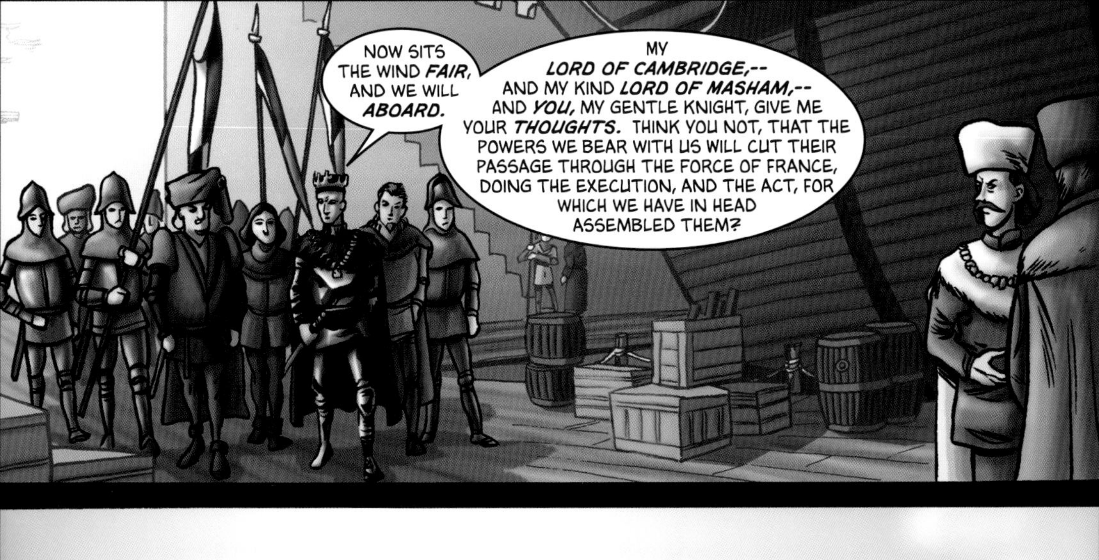
NOW SITS THE WIND FAIR, AND WE WILL ABOARD.
MY LORD OF CAMBRIDGE,-- AND MY KIND LORD OF MASHAM,-- AND YOU, MY GENTLE KNIGHT, GIVE ME YOUR THOUGHTS. THINK YOU NOT, THAT THE POWERS WE BEAR WITH US WILL CUT THEIR PASSAGE THROUGH THE FORCE OF FRANCE, DOING THE EXECUTION, AND THE ACT, FOR WHICH WE HAVE IN HEAD ASSEMBLED THEM?

NO DOUBT, MY LIEGE, IF EACH MAN DO HIS BEST.
I DOUBT NOT THAT: SINCE WE ARE WELL PERSUADED, WE CARRY NOT A HEART WITH US FROM HENCE, THAT GROWS NOT IN A FAIR CONSENT WITH OURS; NOR LEAVE NOT ONE BEHIND, THAT DOTH NOT WISH SUCCESS AND CONQUEST TO ATTEND ON US.
NEVER WAS MONARCH BETTER FEAR'D AND LOV'D THAN IS YOUR MAJESTY: THERE'S NOT, I THINK, A SUBJECT, THAT SITS IN HEART-GRIEF AND UNEASINESS UNDER THE SWEET SHADE OF YOUR GOVERNMENT.
TRUE: THOSE THAT WERE YOUR FATHER'S ENEMIES HAVE STEEP'D THEIR GALLS IN HONEY, AND DO SERVE YOU WITH HEARTS CREATE OF DUTY AND OF ZEAL.
WE THEREFORE HAVE GREAT CAUSE OF THANKFULNESS, AND SHALL FORGET THE OFFICE OF OUR HAND, SOONER THAN QUITTANCE OF DESERT AND MERIT, ACCORDING TO THE WEIGHT AND WORTHINESS.
SO SERVICE SHALL WITH STEELED SINEWS TOIL, AND LABOUR SHALL REFRESH ITSELF WITH HOPE, TO DO YOUR GRACE INCESSANT SERVICES.
WE JUDGE NO LESS.
UNCLE OF EXETER, ENLARGE THE MAN COMMITTED YESTERDAY, THAT RAIL'D AGAINST OUR PERSON: WE CONSIDER, IT WAS EXCESS OF WINE THAT SET HIM ON; AND, ON HIS MORE ADVICE, WE PARDON HIM.
THAT'S MERCY, BUT TOO MUCH SECURITY:
LET HIM BE PUNISH'D, SOVEREIGN; LEST EXAMPLE BREED, BY HIS SUFFERANCE, MORE OF SUCH A KIND.

O, LET US YET BE MERCIFUL.
SO MAY YOUR HIGHNESS, AND YET PUNISH TOO.
SIR, YOU SHOW GREAT MERCY, IF YOU GIVE HIM LIFE AFTER THE TASTE OF MUCH CORRECTION.
ALAS! YOUR TOO MUCH LOVE AND CARE OF ME ARE HEAVY ORISONS 'GAINST THIS POOR WRETCH!
IF LITTLE FAULTS, PROCEEDING ON DISTEMPER, SHALL NOT BE WINK'D AT, HOW SHALL WE STRETCH OUR EYE, WHEN CAPITAL CRIMES, CHEW'D, SWALLOW'D AND DIGESTED, APPEAR BEFORE US? WE'LL YET ENLARGE THAT MAN, THOUGH CAMBRIDGE, SCROOP, AND GREY, IN THEIR DEAR CARE AND TENDER PRESERVATION OF OUR PERSON, WOULD HAVE HIM PUNISH'D.
AND NOW TO OUR FRENCH CAUSES: WHO ARE THE LATE COMMISSIONERS?
I ONE, MY LORD. YOUR HIGHNESS BADE ME ASK FOR IT TO-DAY.
SO DID YOU ME, MY LIEGE.
AND I, MY ROYAL SOVEREIGN.

THEN, RICHARD EARL OF CAMBRIDGE, THERE IS YOURS; -- THERE YOURS, LORD SCROOP OF MASHAM; -- AND, SIR KNIGHT, GREY OF NORTHUMBERLAND, THIS SAME IS YOURS: --
READ THEM; AND KNOW, I KNOW YOUR WORTHINESS.

MY LORD OF WESTMORELAND, AND UNCLE EXETER, WE WILL ABOARD TO-NIGHT.

WHY, HOW NOW, GENTLEMEN? WHAT SEE YOU IN THOSE PAPERS THAT YOU LOSE SO MUCH COMPLEXION? -- LOOK YE, HOW THEY CHANGE! THEIR CHEEKS ARE PAPER. -- WHY, WHAT READ YOU THERE, THAT HAVE SO COWARDED AND CHAS'D YOUR BLOOD OUT OF APPEARANCE?
I DO CONFESS MY FAULT, AND DO SUBMIT ME TO YOUR HIGHNESS' MERCY.
TO WHICH WE ALL APPEAL.

THE MERCY THAT WAS QUICK IN US BUT LATE BY YOUR OWN COUNSEL IS SUPPRESS'D AND KILL'D: YOU MUST NOT DARE, FOR SHAME, TO TALK OF MERCY; FOR YOUR OWN REASONS TURN INTO YOUR BOSOMS, AS DOGS UPON THEIR MASTERS, WORRYING YOU.
SEE YOU, MY PRINCES AND MY NOBLE PEERS, THESE ENGLISH MONSTERS!

MY LORD OF CAMBRIDGE HERE, YOU KNOW HOW APT OUR LOVE WAS, TO ACCORD TO FURNISH HIM WITH AN APPERTINENTS BELONGING TO HIS HONOUR; AND THIS MAN HATH, FOR A FEW LIGHT CROWNS, LIGHTLY CONSPIR'D, AND SWORN UNTO THE PRACTISES OF FRANCE, TO KILL US HERE IN HAMPTON:
TO THE WHICH, THIS KNIGHT, NO LESS FOR BOUNTY BOUND TO US THAN CAMBRIDGE IS, HATH LIKEWISE SWORN.
BUT, O! WHAT SHALL I SAY TO THEE, LORD SCROOP? THOU CRUEL, INGRATEFUL, SAVAGE, AND INHUMAN CREATURE!
THOU THAT DIDST BEAR THE KEY OF ALL MY COUNSELS, THAT KNEW'ST THE VERY BOTTOM OF MY SOUL, THAT ALMOST MIGHTST HAVE COIN'D ME INTO GOLD, WOULDST THOU HAVE PRACTIS'D ON ME FOR THY USE! MAY IT BE POSSIBLE, THAT FOREIGN HIRE COULD OUT OF THEE EXTRACT ONE SPARK OF EVIL, THAT MIGHT ANNOY MY FINGER?
'TIS SO STRANGE, THAT, THOUGH THE TRUTH OF IT STANDS OFF AS GROSS AS BLACK AND WHITE, MY EYE WILL SCARCELY SEE IT.
TREASON AND MURDER EVER KEPT TOGETHER, AS TWO YOKE-DEVILS SWORN TO EITHER'S PURPOSE, WORKING SO GROSSLY IN A NATURAL CAUSE, THAT ADMIRATION DID NOT WHOOP AT THEM; BUT THOU, 'GAINST ALL PROPORTION, DIDST BRING IN WONDER TO WAIT ON TREASON, AND ON MURDER;
AND WHATSOEVER CUNNING FIEND IT WAS, THAT WROUGHT UPON THEE SO PREPOSTEROUSLY, HATH GOT THE VOICE IN HELL FOR EXCELLENCE:
AND OTHER DEVILS, THAT SUGGEST BY TREASONS, DO BOTCH AND BUNGLE UP DAMNATION WITH PATCHES, COLOURS, AND WITH FORMS, BEING FETCH'D FROM GLIST'RING SEMBLANCES OF PIETY;
BUT HE THAT TEMPER'D THEE BADE THEE STAND UP, GAVE THEE NO INSTANCE WHY THOU SHOULDST DO TREASON, UNLESS TO DUB THEE WITH THE NAME OF TRAITOR.

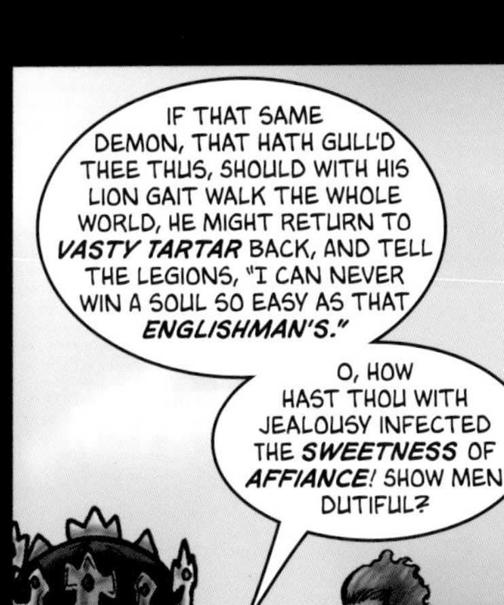
IF THAT SAME DEMON, THAT HATH GULL'D THEE THUS, SHOULD WITH HIS LION GAIT WALK THE WHOLE WORLD, HE MIGHT RETURN TO VASTY TARTAR BACK, AND TELL THE LEGIONS, "I CAN NEVER WIN A SOUL SO EASY AS THAT ENGLISHMAN'S."
O, HOW HAST THOU WITH JEALOUSY INFECTED THE SWEETNESS OF AFFIANCE! SHOW MEN DUTIFUL?

WHY, SO DIDST THOU: SEEM THEY GRAVE AND LEARNED? WHY, SO DIDST THOU: COME THEY OF NOBLE FAMILY? WHY, SO DIDST THOU: SEEM THEY RELIGIOUS? WHY, SO DIDST THOU:
OR ARE THEY SPARE IN DIET; FREE FROM GROSS PASSION, OR OF MIRTH, OR ANGER; CONSTANT IN SPIRIT, NOT SWERVING WITH THE BLOOD; GARNISH'D AND DECK'D IN MODEST COMPLEMENT, NOT WORKING WITH THE EYE WITHOUT THE EAR, AND BUT IN PURGED JUDGMENT TRUSTING NEITHER?
SUCH, AND SO FINELY BOLTED, DIDST THOU SEEM; AND THUS THY FALL HATH LEFT A KIND OF BLOT, TO MARK THE FULL-FRAUGHT MAN AND BEST INDUED, WITH SOME SUSPICION. I WILL WEEP FOR THEE;
FOR THIS REVOLT OF THINE, METHINKS, IS LIKE ANOTHER FALL OF MAN.

THEIR FAULTS ARE OPEN:
ARREST THEM TO THE ANSWER OF THE LAW; AND GOD ACQUIT THEM OF THEIR PRACTISES!

I ARREST THEE OF HIGH TREASON, BY THE NAME OF RICHARD EARL OF CAMBRIDGE.
I ARREST THEE OF HIGH TREASON, BY THE NAME OF HENRY LORD SCROOP OF MASHAM.
I ARREST THEE OF HIGH TREASON, BY THE NAME OF THOMAS GREY, KNIGHT, OF NORTHUMBERLAND.

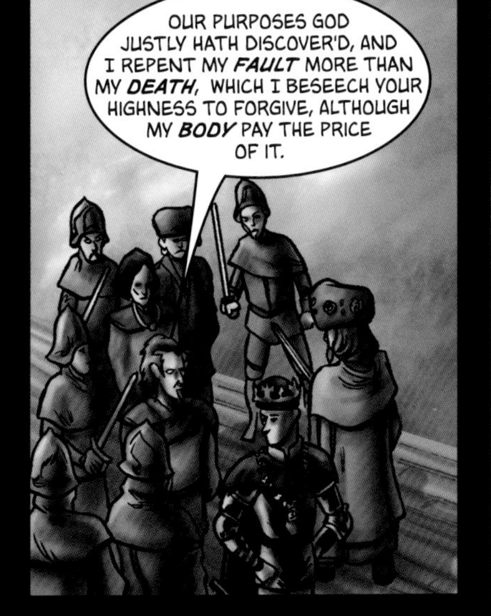
OUR PURPOSES GOD JUSTLY HATH DISCOVER'D, AND I REPENT MY FAULT MORE THAN MY DEATH, WHICH I BESEECH YOUR HIGHNESS TO FORGIVE, ALTHOUGH MY BODY PAY THE PRICE OF IT.

FOR ME, -- THE GOLD OF FRANCE DID NOT SEDUCE, ALTHOUGH I DID ADMIT IT AS A MOTIVE, THE SOONER TO EFFECT WHAT I INTENDED. BUT GOD BE THANKED FOR PREVENTION; WHICH I IN SUFFERANCE HEARTILY WILL REJOICE, BESEECHING GOD AND YOU TO PARDON ME.
NEVER DID FAITHFUL SUBJECT MORE REJOICE AT THE DISCOVERY OF MOST DANGEROUS TREASON, THAN I DO AT THIS HOUR JOY O'ER MYSELF, PREVENTED FROM A DAMNED ENTERPRISE. MY FAULT, BUT NOT MY BODY, PARDON, SOVEREIGN.

GOD QUIT YOU IN HIS MERCY! HEAR YOUR SENTENCE. YOU HAVE CONSPIR'D AGAINST OUR ROYAL PERSON, JOIN'D WITH AN ENEMY PROCLAIM'D, AND FROM HIS COFFERS RECEIVED THE GOLDEN EARNEST OF OUR DEATH;
WHEREIN YOU WOULD HAVE SOLD YOUR KING TO SLAUGHTER, HIS PRINCES AND HIS PEERS TO SERVITUDE, HIS SUBJECTS TO OPPRESSION AND CONTEMPT, AND HIS WHOLE KINGDOM INTO DESOLATION.

TOUCHING OUR PERSON, SEEK WE NO REVENGE; BUT WE OUR KINGDOM'S SAFETY MUST SO TENDER, WHOSE RUIN YOU HAVE SOUGHT, THAT TO HER LAWS WE DO DELIVER YOU. GET YOU THEREFORE HENCE, POOR MISERABLE WRETCHES, TO YOUR DEATH;
THE TASTE WHEREOF, GOD, OF HIS MERCY, GIVE YOU PATIENCE TO ENDURE, AND TRUE REPENTANCE OF ALL YOUR DEAR OFFENCES!
BEAR THEM HENCE!

NOW, LORDS, FOR FRANCE; THE ENTERPRISE WHEREOF SHALL BE TO YOU, AS US, LIKE GLORIOUS.

WE DOUBT NOT OF A FAIR AND LUCKY WAR, SINCE GOD SO GRACIOUSLY HATH BROUGHT TO LIGHT THIS DANGEROUS TREASON LURKING IN OUR WAY TO HINDER OUR BEGINNINGS: WE DOUBT NOT NOW BUT EVERY RUB IS SMOOTHED ON OUR WAY.
THEN FORTH, DEAR COUNTRYMEN! LET US DELIVER OUR PUISSANCE INTO THE HAND OF GOD, PUTTING IT STRAIGHT IN EXPEDITION. CHEERLY TO SEA! THE SIGNS OF WAR ADVANCE!
NO KING OF ENGLAND, IF NOT KING OF FRANCE!

Act Two
Scene Three
LONDON - THE BOARS HEAD TAVERN, IN EASTCHEAP - SUMMER 1415...
PR'YTHEE, HONEY-SWEET HUSBAND, LET ME BRING THEE TO STAINES.
NO; FOR MY MANLY HEART DOTH YEARN.
BARDOLPH, BE BLITHE; NYM, ROUSE THY VAUNTING VEINS; BOY, BRISTLE THY COURAGE UP; FOR FALSTAFF HE IS DEAD, AND WE MUST YEARN THEREFORE.
'WOULD I WERE WITH HIM, WHERESOME'ER HE IS, EITHER IN HEAVEN OR IN HELL!

NAY, SURE, HE'S NOT IN HELL: HE'S IN ARTHUR'S BOSOM, IF EVER MAN WENT TO ARTHUR'S BOSOM. 'A MADE A FINER END AND WENT AWAY AN IT HAD BEEN ANY CHRISTOM CHILD; 'A PARTED EVEN JUST BETWEEN TWELVE AND ONE, EVEN AT THE TURNING O' THE TIDE:
FOR AFTER I SAW HIM FUMBLE WITH THE SHEETS AND PLAY WITH FLOWERS AND SMILE UPON HIS FINGERS' ENDS, I KNEW THERE WAS BUT ONE WAY; FOR HIS NOSE WAS AS SHARP AS A PEN, AND A TABLE OF GREEN FIELDS.

"HOW NOW, SIR JOHN?" QUOTH I; "WHAT, MAN! BE O' GOOD CHEER." SO 'A CRIED OUT, "GOD, GOD, GOD!" THREE OR FOUR TIMES:
NOW I, TO COMFORT HIM, BID HIM, 'A SHOULD NOT THINK OF GOD; I HOP'D THERE WAS NO NEED TO TROUBLE HIMSELF WITH ANY SUCH THOUGHTS YET. SO 'A BADE ME LAY MORE CLOTHES ON HIS FEET. I PUT MY HAND INTO THE BED AND FELT THEM, AND THEY WERE AS COLD AS ANY STONE; THEN I FELT TO HIS KNEES, AND SO UPWARD AND UPWARD, AND ALL WAS AS COLD AS ANY STONE.

THEY SAY HE CRIED OUT OF SACK.
AY, THAT 'A DID.
AND OF WOMEN.
NAY, THAT 'A DID NOT.
YES, THAT 'A DID; AND SAID THEY WERE DEVILS INCARNATE.

'A COULD NEVER ABIDE CARNATION; 'TWAS A COLOUR HE NEVER LIKED.
'A SAID ONCE, THE DEVIL WOULD HAVE HIM ABOUT WOMEN.
'A DID IN SOME SORT, INDEED, HANDLE WOMEN; BUT THEN HE WAS RHEUMATIC, AND TALKED OF THE WHORE OF BABYLON.
DO YOU NOT REMEMBER, 'A SAW A FLEA STICK UPON BARDOLPH'S NOSE, AND 'A SAID IT WAS A BLACK SOUL BURNING IN HELL-FIRE?

WELL, THE FUEL IS GONE THAT MAINTAIN'D THAT FIRE; THAT'S ALL THE RICHES I GOT IN HIS SERVICE.
SHALL WE SHOG? THE KING WILL BE GONE FROM SOUTHAMPTON.

COME, LET'S AWAY. -- MY LOVE, GIVE ME THY LIPS.
LOOK TO MY CHATTELS AND MY MOVABLES. LET SENSES RULE; THE WORD IS "PITCH AND PAY." TRUST NONE; FOR OATHS ARE STRAWS, MEN'S FAITHS ARE WAFER-CAKES AND HOLD-FAST IS THE ONLY DOG, MY DUCK; THEREFORE, CAVETO BE THY COUNSELLOR. GO, CLEAR THY CRYSTALS.

YOKE-FELLOWS IN ARMS, LET US TO FRANCE; LIKE HORSE-LEECHES, MY BOYS, TO SUCK, TO SUCK, THE VERY BLOOD TO SUCK!
AND THAT'S BUT UNWHOLESOME FOOD, THEY SAY.
TOUCH HER SOFT MOUTH, AND MARCH.

FAREWELL, HOSTESS.
I CANNOT KISS; THAT IS THE HUMOUR OF IT; BUT, ADIEU.

LET HOUSEWIFERY APPEAR; KEEP CLOSE, I THEE COMMAND.
FAREWELL; ADIEU.

Act Two
Scene Four

WELL, 'TIS NOT SO, MY LORD HIGH CONSTABLE; BUT THOUGH WE THINK IT SO, IT IS NO MATTER.
IN CASES OF DEFENCE 'TIS BEST TO WEIGH THE ENEMY MORE MIGHTY THAN HE SEEMS, SO THE PROPORTIONS OF DEFENCE ARE FILL'D; WHICH, OF A WEAK AND NIGGARDLY PROJECTION, DOTH, LIKE A MISER, SPOIL HIS COAT WITH SCANTING A LITTLE CLOTH.
THINK WE KING HARRY STRONG; AND, PRINCES, LOOK YOU STRONGLY ARM TO MEET HIM.

THE KINDRED OF HIM HATH BEEN FLESH'D UPON US; AND HE IS BRED OUT OF THAT BLOODY STRAIN THAT HAUNTED US IN OUR FAMILIAR PATHS. WITNESS OUR TOO MUCH MEMORABLE SHAME WHEN CRESSY BATTLE FATALLY WAS STRUCK, AND ALL OUR PRINCES CAPTIV'D BY THE HAND OF THAT BLACK NAME, EDWARD, BLACK PRINCE OF WALES;
WHILES THAT HIS MOUNTAIN SIRE, -- ON MOUNTAIN STANDING, UP IN THE AIR, CROWN'D WITH THE GOLDEN SUN, -- SAW HIS HEROICAL SEED, AND SMIL'D TO SEE HIM, MANGLE THE WORK OF NATURE AND DEFACE THE PATTERNS THAT BY GOD AND BY FRENCH FATHERS HAD TWENTY YEARS BEEN MADE. THIS IS A STEM OF THAT VICTORIOUS STOCK; AND LET US FEAR THE NATIVE MIGHTINESS AND FATE OF HIM.

AMBASSADORS FROM HARRY, KING OF ENGLAND, DO CRAVE ADMITTANCE TO YOUR MAJESTY.
WE'LL GIVE THEM PRESENT AUDIENCE. GO, AND BRING THEM.
YOU SEE, THIS CHASE IS HOTLY FOLLOW'D, FRIENDS.
TURN HEAD, AND STOP PURSUIT; FOR COWARD DOGS MOST SPEND THEIR MOUTHS, WHEN WHAT THEY SEEM TO THREATEN RUNS FAR BEFORE THEM. GOOD MY SOVEREIGN, TAKE UP THE ENGLISH SHORT, AND LET THEM KNOW OF WHAT A MONARCHY YOU ARE THE HEAD:
SELF-LOVE, MY LIEGE, IS NOT SO VILE A SIN AS SELF-NEGLECTING.

FROM OUR BROTHER ENGLAND?
FROM HIM; AND THUS HE **GREETS** YOUR MAJESTY:
HE **WILLS** YOU, IN THE NAME OF GOD ALMIGHTY, THAT YOU DIVEST YOURSELF, AND LAY APART THE BORROW'D GLORIES, THAT BY GIFT OF HEAVEN, BY LAW OF NATURE, AND OF NATIONS, 'LONG TO **HIM,** AND TO HIS **HEIRS**;
NAMELY, THE CROWN, AND ALL WIDE-STRETCHED HONOURS THAT PERTAIN, BY CUSTOM AND THE ORDINANCE OF TIMES, UNTO THE **CROWN OF FRANCE.**
THAT YOU MAY KNOW, 'TIS NO **SINISTER** NOR NO **AWKWARD** CLAIM PICK'D FROM THE WORM-HOLES OF LONG-VANISH'D DAYS, NOR FROM THE DUST OF OLD OBLIVION RAK'D, HE SENDS YOU THIS MOST **MEMORABLE** LINE, IN EVERY BRANCH TRULY **DEMONSTRATIVE**; WILLING YOU OVERLOOK THIS PEDIGREE;
AND WHEN YOU FIND HIM EVENLY DERIV'D FROM HIS MOST FAM'D OF FAMOUS ANCESTORS, **EDWARD THE THIRD**, HE BIDS YOU THEN **RESIGN** YOUR CROWN AND KINGDOM, INDIRECTLY HELD FROM HIM, THE **NATIVE** AND **TRUE** CHALLENGER.
OR ELSE WHAT FOLLOWS?
BLOODY CONSTRAINT; FOR IF YOU HIDE THE CROWN EVEN IN YOUR **HEARTS**, THERE WILL HE RAKE FOR IT.
THEREFORE IN **FIERCE TEMPEST** IS HE COMING, IN **THUNDER** AND IN **EARTHQUAKE**, LIKE A JOVE, THAT, IF REQUIRING **FAIL**, HE WILL **COMPEL;** AND BIDS YOU, IN THE BOWELS OF THE LORD, DELIVER UP THE CROWN, AND TO TAKE MERCY ON THE POOR SOULS FOR WHOM THIS **HUNGRY WAR** OPENS HIS **VASTY JAWS**; AND ON YOUR HEAD TURNING THE **WIDOWS' TEARS**, THE **ORPHANS' CRIES** THE **DEAD MEN'S BLOOD**, THE **PINING MAIDENS' GROANS**, FOR **HUSBANDS**, **FATHERS,** AND **BETROTHED LOVERS**, THAT SHALL BE **SWALLOW'D** IN THIS CONTROVERSY.
THIS IS HIS CLAIM, HIS THREAT'NING, AND MY MESSAGE; UNLESS THE **DAUPHIN** BE IN PRESENCE HERE, TO WHOM EXPRESSLY I BRING GREETING **TOO.**

FOR US, WE WILL CONSIDER OF THIS FURTHER. TO-MORROW SHALL YOU BEAR OUR FULL INTENT BACK TO OUR BROTHER ENGLAND.

FOR THE DAUPHIN, I STAND HERE FOR HIM. WHAT TO HIM FROM ENGLAND?
SCORN AND DEFIANCE, SLIGHT REGARD, CONTEMPT, AND ANYTHING THAT MAY NOT MISBECOME THE MIGHTY SENDER, DOTH HE PRIZE YOU AT.
THUS SAYS MY KING: AN IF YOUR FATHER'S HIGHNESS DO NOT, IN GRANT OF ALL DEMANDS AT LARGE, SWEETEN THE BITTER MOCK YOU SENT HIS MAJESTY, HE'LL CALL YOU TO SO HOT AN ANSWER OF IT, THAT CAVES AND WOMBY VAULTAGES OF FRANCE SHALL CHIDE YOUR TRESPASS AND RETURN YOUR MOCK IN SECOND ACCENT OF HIS ORDINANCE.

SAY, IF MY FATHER RENDER FAIR RETURN, IT IS AGAINST MY WILL; FOR I DESIRE NOTHING BUT ODDS WITH ENGLAND: TO THAT END, AS MATCHING TO HIS YOUTH AND VANITY, I DID PRESENT HIM WITH THE PARIS BALLS.
HE'LL MAKE YOUR PARIS LOUVRE SHAKE FOR IT, WERE IT THE MISTRESS-COURT OF MIGHTY EUROPE;
AND, BE ASSURED, YOU'LL FIND A DIFFERENCE, AS WE, HIS SUBJECTS, HAVE IN WONDER FOUND, BETWEEN THE PROMISE OF HIS GREENER DAYS, AND THESE HE MASTERS NOW. NOW HE WEIGHS TIME EVEN TO THE UTMOST GRAIN; THAT YOU SHALL READ IN YOUR OWN LOSSES, IF HE STAY IN FRANCE.
TO-MORROW SHALL YOU KNOW OUR MIND AT FULL.
DISPATCH US WITH ALL SPEED, LEST THAT OUR KING COME HERE HIMSELF TO QUESTION OUR DELAY; FOR HE IS FOOTED IN THIS LAND ALREADY.
YOU SHALL BE SOON DISPATCH'D WITH FAIR CONDITIONS. A NIGHT IS BUT SMALL BREATH AND LITTLE PAUSE TO ANSWER MATTERS OF THIS CONSEQUENCE.

Act Three
Prologue
THUS WITH IMAGIN'D WING OUR SWIFT SCENE FLIES, IN MOTION OF NO LESS CELERITY THAN THAT OF THOUGHT. SUPPOSE THAT YOU HAVE SEEN THE WELL-APPOINTED KING AT HAMPTON PIER EMBARK HIS ROYALTY, AND HIS BRAVE FLEET WITH SILKEN STREAMERS THE YOUNG PHOEBUS FANNING.
PLAY WITH YOUR FANCIES, AND IN THEM BEHOLD UPON THE HEMPEN TACKLE SHIP-BOYS CLIMBING;
HEAR THE SHRILL WHISTLE, WHICH DOTH ORDER GIVE TO SOUNDS CONFUS'D; BEHOLD THE THREADEN SAILS, BORNE WITH THE INVISIBLE AND CREEPING WIND, DRAW THE HUGE BOTTOMS THROUGH THE FURROW'D SEA, BREASTING THE LOFTY SURGE.
O! DO BUT THINK, YOU STAND UPON THE RIVAGE AND BEHOLD A CITY ON THE INCONSTANT BILLOWS DANCING;

FOR SO APPEARS THIS FLEET MAJESTICAL, HOLDING DUE COURSE TO HARFLEUR.
FOLLOW, FOLLOW!

GRAPPLE YOUR MINDS TO STERNAGE OF THIS NAVY, AND LEAVE YOUR ENGLAND, AS DEAD MIDNIGHT STILL, GUARDED WITH GRANDSIRES, BABIES, AND OLD WOMEN, EITHER PAST OR NOT ARRIV'D TO PITH AND PUISSANCE.

FOR WHO IS HE, WHOSE CHIN IS BUT ENRICH'D WITH ONE APPEARING HAIR, THAT WILL NOT FOLLOW THESE CULL'D AND CHOICE-DRAWN CAVALIERS TO FRANCE?

WORK, WORK YOUR THOUGHTS, AND THEREIN SEE A SIEGE;
BEHOLD THE ORDNANCE ON THEIR CARRIAGES, WITH FATAL MOUTHS GAPING ON GIRDED HARFLEUR.

SUPPOSE THE AMBASSADOR FROM THE FRENCH COMES BACK, TELLS HARRY THAT THE KING DOTH OFFER HIM KATHERINE HIS DAUGHTER, AND WITH HER, TO DOWRY, SOME PETTY AND UNPROFITABLE DUKEDOMS.
THE OFFER LIKES NOT; AND THE NIMBLE GUNNER WITH LINSTOCK NOW THE DEVILISH CANNON TOUCHES,
AND DOWN GOES ALL BEFORE THEM.

STILL BE KIND, AND EKE OUT OUR PERFORMANCE WITH YOUR MIND.

Act Three
Scene One
FRANCE - HARFLEUR - SEPTEMBER 1415. KING HENRY V HAS THE CITY UNDER SIEGE...
ONCE MORE UNTO THE BREACH, DEAR FRIENDS, ONCE MORE, OR CLOSE THE WALL UP WITH OUR ENGLISH DEAD!

IN PEACE, THERE'S NOTHING SO BECOMES A MAN AS MODEST STILLNESS AND HUMILITY; BUT WHEN THE BLAST OF WAR BLOWS IN OUR EARS, THEN IMITATE THE ACTION OF THE TIGER;
STIFFEN THE SINEWS, SUMMON UP THE BLOOD, DISGUISE FAIR NATURE WITH HARD-FAVOUR'D RAGE; THEN LEND THE EYE A TERRIBLE ASPECT;
LET IT PRY THROUGH THE PORTAGE OF THE HEAD LIKE THE BRASS CANNON; LET THE BROW O'ERWHELM IT AS FEARFULLY AS DOES A GALLED ROCK O'ERHANG AND JUTTY HIS CONFOUNDED BASE, SWILL'D WITH THE WILD AND WASTEFUL OCEAN.

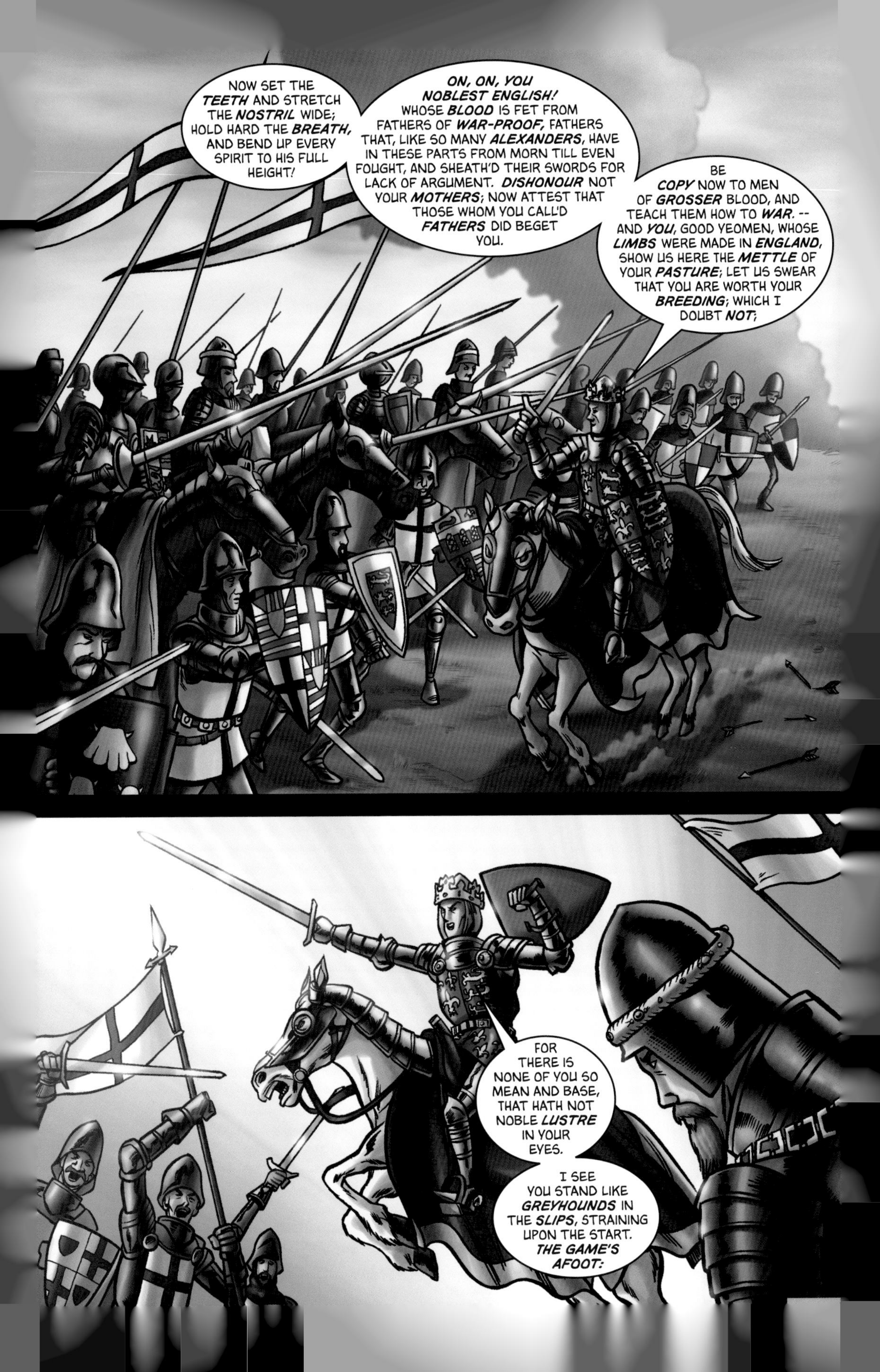
NOW SET THE TEETH AND STRETCH THE NOSTRIL WIDE; HOLD HARD THE BREATH, AND BEND UP EVERY SPIRIT TO HIS FULL HEIGHT!
ON, ON, YOU NOBLEST ENGLISH! WHOSE BLOOD IS FET FROM FATHERS OF WAR-PROOF, FATHERS THAT, LIKE SO MANY ALEXANDERS, HAVE IN THESE PARTS FROM MORN TILL EVEN FOUGHT, AND SHEATH'D THEIR SWORDS FOR LACK OF ARGUMENT. DISHONOUR NOT YOUR MOTHERS; NOW ATTEST THAT THOSE WHOM YOU CALL'D FATHERS DID BEGET YOU.
BE COPY NOW TO MEN OF GROSSER BLOOD, AND TEACH THEM HOW TO WAR. -- AND YOU, GOOD YEOMEN, WHOSE LIMBS WERE MADE IN ENGLAND, SHOW US HERE THE METTLE OF YOUR PASTURE; LET US SWEAR THAT YOU ARE WORTH YOUR BREEDING; WHICH I DOUBT NOT;
FOR THERE IS NONE OF YOU SO MEAN AND BASE, THAT HATH NOT NOBLE LUSTRE IN YOUR EYES.
I SEE YOU STAND LIKE GREYHOUNDS IN THE SLIPS, STRAINING UPON THE START. THE GAME'S AFOOT:

FOLLOW YOUR *SPIRIT*; AND UPON THIS CHARGE,
CRY *"GOD FOR HARRY! ENGLAND AND SAINT GEORGE!"*

Act Three
Scene Two
FRANCE - NEAR THE CITY OF HARFLEUR - SEPTEMBER 1415. THE BATTLE OF HARFLEUR CONTINUES...
ON, ON, ON, ON, ON! TO THE BREACH, TO THE BREACH!
PRAY THEE, CORPORAL, STAY: THE KNOCKS ARE TOO HOT; AND FOR MINE OWN PART, I HAVE NOT A CASE OF LIVES: THE HUMOUR OF IT IS TOO HOT; THAT IS THE VERY PLAIN-SONG OF IT.
THE PLAIN-SONG IS MOST JUST, FOR HUMOURS DO ABOUND;
"KNOCKS GO AND COME; GOD'S VASSALS DROP AND DIE; AND SWORD AND SHIELD, IN BLOODY FIELD, DOTH WIN IMMORTAL FAME."
WOULD I WERE IN AN ALEHOUSE IN LONDON! I WOULD GIVE ALL MY FAME FOR A POT OF ALE, AND SAFETY.
AND I.
"IF WISHES WOULD PREVAIL WITH ME, MY PURPOSE SHOULD NOT FAIL WITH ME, BUT THITHER WOULD I HIE."
"AS DULY, BUT NOT AS TRULY, AS BIRD DOTH SING ON BOUGH."
UP TO THE BREACH, YOU DOGS! AVAUNT, YOU CULLIONS!
BE MERCIFUL, GREAT DUKE, TO MEN OF MOULD! ABATE THY RAGE, ABATE THY MANLY RAGE; ABATE THY RAGE, GREAT DUKE! GOOD BAWCOCK, BATE THY RAGE; USE LENITY, SWEET CHUCK!

THESE BE GOOD HUMOURS! YOUR HONOUR WINS BAD HUMOURS.
AS YOUNG AS I AM, I HAVE OBSERV'D THESE THREE SWASHERS. I AM BOY TO THEM ALL THREE, BUT ALL THEY THREE, THOUGH THEY WOULD SERVE ME, COULD NOT BE MAN TO ME; FOR INDEED THREE SUCH ANTICS DO NOT AMOUNT TO A MAN.
FOR BARDOLPH, HE IS WHITE-LIVERED AND RED-FACED; BY THE MEANS WHEREOF 'A FACES IT OUT, BUT FIGHTS NOT.
FOR PISTOL, HE HATH A KILLING TONGUE AND A QUIET SWORD; BY THE MEANS WHEREOF 'A BREAKS WORDS, AND KEEPS WHOLE WEAPONS.
FOR NYM, HE HATH HEARD THAT MEN OF FEW WORDS ARE THE BEST MEN; AND THEREFORE HE SCORNS TO SAY HIS PRAYERS, LEST 'A SHOULD BE THOUGHT A COWARD: BUT HIS FEW BAD WORDS ARE MATCH'D WITH AS FEW GOOD DEEDS; FOR 'A NEVER BROKE ANY MAN'S HEAD BUT HIS OWN, AND THAT WAS AGAINST A POST WHEN HE WAS DRUNK.
THEY WILL STEAL ANYTHING, AND CALL IT PURCHASE. BARDOLPH STOLE A LUTE-CASE, BORE IT TWELVE LEAGUES, AND SOLD IT FOR THREE HALF-PENCE. NYM AND BARDOLPH ARE SWORN BROTHERS IN FILCHING, AND IN CALAIS THEY STOLE A FIRE-SHOVEL; I KNEW, BY THAT PIECE OF SERVICE, THE MEN WOULD CARRY COALS.
THEY WOULD HAVE ME AS FAMILIAR WITH MEN'S POCKETS AS THEIR GLOVES OR THEIR HANDKERCHIEFS; WHICH MAKES MUCH AGAINST MY MANHOOD, IF I SHOULD TAKE FROM ANOTHER'S POCKET TO PUT INTO MINE; FOR IT IS PLAIN POCKETING UP OF WRONGS.

I MUST LEAVE THEM, AND SEEK SOME BETTER SERVICE:
THEIR VILLAINY GOES AGAINST MY WEAK STOMACH, AND THEREFORE I MUST CAST IT UP.
CAPTAIN FLUELLEN, YOU MUST COME PRESENTLY TO THE MINES: THE DUKE OF GLOUCESTER WOULD SPEAK WITH YOU.
TO THE MINES! TELL YOU THE DUKE, IT IS NOT SO GOOD TO COME TO THE MINES. FOR, LOOK YOU, THE MINES IS NOT ACCORDING TO THE DISCIPLINES OF THE WAR; THE CONCAVITIES OF IT IS NOT SUFFICIENT;
FOR, LOOK YOU, TH'ATHVERSARY, YOU MAY DISCUSS UNTO THE DUKE, LOOK YOU, IS DIGT HIMSELF FOUR YARD UNDER THE COUNTERMINES.
BY CHESHU, I THINK, 'A WILL PLOW UP ALL, IF THERE IS NOT BETTER DIRECTIONS.
THE DUKE OF GLOUCESTER, TO WHOM THE ORDER OF THE SIEGE IS GIVEN, IS ALTOGETHER DIRECTED BY AN IRISHMAN; A VERY VALIANT GENTLEMAN, I' FAITH.
IT IS CAPTAIN MACMORRIS, IS IT NOT?
I THINK IT BE.
BY CHESHU, HE IS AN ASS, AS IN THE WORLD. I WILL VERIFY AS MUCH IN HIS BEARD: HE HAS NO MORE DIRECTIONS IN THE TRUE DISCIPLINES OF THE WARS, LOOK YOU, OF THE ROMAN DISCIPLINES, THAN IS A PUPPY-DOG.

HERE 'A COMES; AND THE SCOTS CAPTAIN, CAPTAIN JAMY, WITH HIM.
CAPTAIN JAMY IS A MARVELLOUS FALOROUS GENTLEMAN, THAT IS CERTAIN; AND OF GREAT EXPEDITION AND KNOWLEDGE IN TH'ANCHIENT WARS, UPON MY PARTICULAR KNOWLEDGE OF HIS DIRECTIONS.
BY CHESHU, HE WILL MAINTAIN HIS ARGUMENT AS WELL AS ANY MILITARY MAN IN THE WORLD, IN THE DISCIPLINES OF THE PRISTINE WARS OF THE ROMANS.
I SAY GUD-DAY, CAPTAIN FLUELLEN.
GOD-DEN TO YOUR WORSHIP, GOOD CAPTAIN JAMES.
HOW NOW, CAPTAIN MACMORRIS! HAVE YOU QUIT THE MINES? HAVE THE PIONEERS GIVEN O'ER?
BY CHRISH, LA, 'TISH ILL DONE: THE WORK ISH GIVE OVER, THE TRUMPET SOUND THE RETREAT. BY MY HAND I SWEAR, AND MY FATHER'S SOUL, THE WORK ISH ILL DONE;
IT ISH GIVE OVER. I WOULD HAVE BLOWED UP THE TOWN, SO CHRISH SAVE ME, LA, IN AN HOUR. O! 'TISH ILL DONE, 'TISH ILL DONE; BY MY HAND, 'TISH ILL DONE.
CAPTAIN MACMORRIS, I BESEECH YOU NOW, WILL YOU VOUCHSAFE ME, LOOK YOU, A FEW DISPUTATIONS WITH YOU, AS PARTLY TOUCHING OR CONCERNING THE DISCIPLINES OF THE WAR, THE ROMAN WARS, IN THE WAY OF ARGUMENT, LOOK YOU, AND FRIENDLY COMMUNICATION;
PARTLY TO SATISFY MY OPINION, AND PARTLY FOR THE SATISFACTION, LOOK YOU, OF MY MIND, AS TOUCHING THE DIRECTION OF THE MILITARY DISCIPLINE; THAT IS THE POINT.
IT SALL BE VARY GUD, GUD FEITH, GUD CAPTAINS BATH: AND I SALL QUIT YOU WITH GUD LEVE, AS I MAY PICK OCCASION; THAT SALL I, MARRY.
IT IS NO TIME TO DISCOURSE, SO CHRISH SAVE ME. THE DAY IS HOT, AND THE WEATHER, AND THE WARS, AND THE KING, AND THE DUKES: IT IS NO TIME TO DISCOURSE.
THE TOWN IS BESEECH'D, AND THE TRUMPET CALL US TO THE BREACH, AND WE TALK, AND, BE CHRISH, DO NOTHING. 'TIS SHAME FOR US ALL; SO GOD SA' ME, 'TIS SHAME TO STAND STILL; IT IS SHAME, BY MY HAND;
AND THERE IS THROATS TO BE CUT, AND WORKS TO BE DONE; AND THERE ISH NOTHING DONE, SO CHRISH SA' ME, LA!

BY THE MESS, ERE THEISE EYES OF MINE TAKE THEMSELVES TO SLOMBER, I'LL DE GUD SERVICE, OR I'LL LIG I' THE GRUND FOR IT; AY, OR GO TO DEATH; AND I'LL PAY IT AS VALOROUSLY AS I MAY, THAT SALL I SURELY DO, THAT IS THE BREFF AND THE LONG. MARRY, I WAD FULL FAIN HEARD SOME QUESTION 'TWEEN YOU TWAY.
CAPTAIN MACMORRIS, I THINK, LOOK YOU, UNDER YOUR CORRECTION, THERE IS NOT MANY OF YOUR NATION --
OF MY NATION! WHAT ISH MY NATION? ISH A VILLAIN, AND A BASTARD, AND A KNAVE, AND A RASCAL? WHAT ISH MY NATION? WHO TALKS OF MY NATION?
LOOK YOU, IF YOU TAKE THE MATTER OTHERWISE THAN IS MEANT, CAPTAIN MACMORRIS, PERADVENTURE I SHALL THINK YOU DO NOT USE ME WITH THAT AFFABILITY AS IN DISCRETION YOU OUGHT TO USE ME, LOOK YOU;
BEING AS GOOD A MAN AS YOURSELF, BOTH IN THE DISCIPLINES OF WAR, AND IN THE DERIVATION OF MY BIRTH, AND IN OTHER PARTICULARITIES.
I DO NOT KNOW YOU SO GOOD A MAN AS MYSELF: SO CHRISH SAVE ME, I WILL CUT OFF YOUR HEAD.
GENTLEMEN BOTH, YOU WILL MISTAKE EACH OTHER.
AH! THAT'S A FOUL FAULT.
TAN-TARA!
THE TOWN SOUNDS A PARLEY.
CAPTAIN MACMORRIS, WHEN THERE IS MORE BETTER OPPORTUNITY TO BE REQUIRED, LOOK YOU, I WILL BE SO BOLD AS TO TELL YOU, I KNOW THE DISCIPLINES OF WAR; AND THERE IS AN END.
TAN-TARA!
TAN-TARA!

Act Three
Scene Three
FRANCE - AT THE GATES OF HARFLEUR - 22ND SEPTEMBER 1415. THE BATTLE HAS PAUSED...
HOW YET RESOLVES THE GOVERNOR OF THE TOWN? THIS IS THE LATEST PARLE WE WILL ADMIT; THEREFORE, TO OUR BEST MERCY GIVE YOURSELVES;
OR, LIKE TO MEN PROUD OF DESTRUCTION, DEFY US TO OUR WORST: FOR, AS I AM A SOLDIER, A NAME THAT IN MY THOUGHTS BECOMES ME BEST, IF I BEGIN THE BATTERY ONCE AGAIN, I WILL NOT LEAVE THE HALF-ACHIEVED HARFLEUR TILL IN HER ASHES SHE LIE BURIED.
THE GATES OF MERCY SHALL BE ALL SHUT UP; AND THE FLESH'D SOLDIER, ROUGH AND HARD OF HEART, IN LIBERTY OF BLOODY HAND SHALL RANGE WITH CONSCIENCE WIDE AS HELL, MOWING LIKE GRASS YOUR FRESH-FAIR VIRGINS AND YOUR FLOW'RING INFANTS.
WHAT IS IT THEN TO ME, IF IMPIOUS WAR, ARRAY'D IN FLAMES LIKE TO THE PRINCE OF FIENDS, DO WITH HIS SMIRCH'D COMPLEXION ALL FELL FEATS ENLINK'D TO WASTE AND DESOLATION?

IF YOUR PURE MAIDENS FALL INTO THE HAND OF HOT AND FORCING VIOLATION?
WHEN DOWN THE HILL HE HOLDS HIS FIERCE CAREER? WE MAY AS BOOTLES SPEND OUR VAIN COMMAND UPON THE ENRAGED SOLDIERS IN THEIR SPOIL, AS SE PRECEPTS TO THE LEVIATHAN TO COM ASHORE. THEREFORE, YOU MEN OF HARFLE TAKE PITY OF YOUR TOWN AND OF YOU PEOPLE, WHILES YET MY SOLDIERS ARE MY COMMAND; WHILES YET THE COOL AN TEMPERATE WIND OF GRACE O'ERBLOV THE FILTHY AND CONTAGIOUS CLOUDS OF HEADY MURDER, SPOIL, AND VILLAINY.
IF NOT, WHY, IN A MOMENT LOOK TO SEE THE BLIND AND BLOODY SOLDIER WITH FOUL HAND DEFILE THE LOCKS OF YOUR SHRILL-SHRIEKING DAUGHTERS;
YOUR FATHERS TAKEN BY THE SILVER BEARDS, AND THEIR MOST REVEREND HEADS DASH'D TO THE WALLS; YOUR NAKED INFANTS SPITTED UPON PIKES, WHILES THE MAD MOTHERS WITH THEIR HOWLS CONFUS'D DO BREAK THE CLOUDS, AS DID THE WIVES OF JEWRY AT HEROD'S BLOODY-HUNTING SLAUGHTERMEN.
WHAT SAY YOU? WILL YOU YIELD, AND THIS AVOID? OR, GUILTY IN DEFENCE, BE THUS DESTROY'D?
OUR EXPECTATION HATH THIS DAY AN END. THE DAUPHIN, WHOM OF SUCCOUR WE ENTREATED, RETURNS US, THAT HIS POWERS ARE YET NOT READY TO RAISE SO GREAT A SIEGE. THEREFORE, GREAT KING, WE YIELD OUR TOWN AND LIVES TO THY SOFT MERCY.
ENTER OUR GATES; DISPOSE OF US AND OURS; FOR WE NO LONGER ARE DEFENSIBLE.
OPEN YOUR GATES!
COME, UNCLE EXETER, GO YOU AND ENTER HARFLEUR; THERE REMAIN, AND FORTIFY IT STRONGLY 'GAINST THE FRENCH.
USE MERCY TO THEM ALL. FOR US, DEAR UNCLE, THE WINTER COMING ON, AND SICKNESS GROWING UPON OUR SOLDIERS, WE WILL RETIRE TO CALAIS.
TO-NIGHT IN HARFLEUR WILL WE BE YOUR GUEST; TO-MORROW FOR THE MARCH ARE WE ADDRESSED.

Act Three
Scene Four
FRANCE - OUTSIDE THE PALACE OF ROUEN. PRINCESS KATHERINE IS TALKING WITH HER MAID...
ALICE, TU AS ÉTÉ EN ANGLETERRE, ET TU BIEN PARLES LE LANGAGE.
UN PEU, MADAME.
JE TE PRIE, M'ENSEIGNEZ; IL FAUT QUE J'APPRENNE À PARLER. COMMENT APPELEZ-VOUS LA MAIN EN ANGLAIS?
LA MAIN? ELLE EST APPELÉE DE HAND.
DE HAND. ET LES DOIGTS?
LES DOIGTS? MA FOI, J'OUBLIE LES DOIGTS; MAIS JE ME SOUVIENDRAI. LES DOIGTS, JE PENSE QU'ILS SONT APPELÉS DE FINGRES; OUI, DE FINGRES.
LA MAIN, DE HAND; LES DOIGTS, DE FINGRES. JE PENSE QUE JE SUIS LE BON ÉCOLIER; J'AI GAGNÉ DEUX MOTS D'ANGLAIS VITEMENT. COMMENT APPELEZ-VOUS LES ONGLES?
LES ONGLES? NOUS LES APPELONS DE NAILS.

DE NAILS. ÉCOUTEZ; DITES-MOI, SI JE PARLE BIEN:
DE HAND, DE FINGRES, ET DE NAILS.
C'EST BIEN DIT, MADAME; IL EST FORT BON ANGLAIS.
DITES-MOI L'ANGLAIS POUR LE BRAS.
DE ARM, MADAME.
ET LE COUDE?
D'ELBOW.

D'ELBOW. JE M'EN FAIS LA RÉPÉTITION DE TOUS LES MOTS QUE VOUS M'AVEZ APPRIS DÈS À PRÉSENT.

IL EST TROP DIFFICILE, MADAME, COMME JE PENSE.
EXCUSEZ-MOI, ALICE; ÉCOUTEZ: D'HAND, DE FINGRES, DE NAILS, D'ARM, DE BILBOW.
D'ELBOW, MADAME.

O SEIGNEUR DIEU, JE M'EN OUBLIE! D'ELBOW. COMMENT APPELEZ-VOUS LE COL?

DE NICK, MADAME.
DE NICK. ET LE MENTON?
DE CHIN.

DE SIN.
LE COL, DE NICK; LE MENTON, DE SIN.
OUI. SAUF VOTRE HONNEUR, EN VÉRITÉ, VOUS PRONONCEZ LES MOTS AUSSI DROIT QUE LES NATIFS D'ANGLETERRE.
JE NE DOUTE POINT D'APPRENDRE, PAR LA GRÂCE DE DIEU, ET EN PEU DE TEMPS.
N'AVEZ VOUS DÉJÀ OUBLIÉ CE QUE JE VOUS AI ENSEIGNÉ?
NON, JE RÉCITERAI À VOUS PROMPTEMENT:
D'HAND, DE FINGRES, DE MAILS...
DE NAILS, MADAME.
DE NAILS, DE ARM, DE ILBOW.
SAUF VOTRE HONNEUR, DE ELBOW.
AINSI DIS-JE; D'ELBOW, DE NICK, ET DE SIN. COMMENT APPELEZ-VOUS LE PIED ET LA ROBE?
DE FOOT, MADAME; ET DE COUN.
DE FOOT ET DE COUN? O SEIGNEUR DIEU,
ILS SONT LES MOTS DE SON MAUVAIS, CORRUPTIBLE, GROS, ET IMPUDIQUE, ET NON POUR LES DAMES D'HONNEUR D'USER: JE NE VOUDRAIS PRONONCER CES MOTS DEVANT LES SEIGNEURS DE FRANCE POUR TOUT LE MONDE.
FOH! DE FOOT ET DE COUN! NÉANMOINS, JE RÉCITERAI UNE AUTRE FOIS MA LEÇON ENSEMBLE:
D'HAND, DE FINGRES, DE NAILS, D'ARM, D'ELBOW, DE NICK, DE SIN, DE FOOT, DE COUN.
EXCELLENT, MADAME!
C'EST ASSEZ POUR UNE FOIS: ALLONS-NOUS À DÎNER.

Act Three
Scene Five
FRANCE - THE PALACE OF ROUEN - 20TH OCTOBER 1415. KING CHARLES VI IS ANGRY WITH THEIR DEFEAT AT HARFLEUR...
'TIS CERTAIN HE HATH PASS'D THE RIVER SOMME.
AND IF HE BE NOT FOUGHT WITHAL, MY LORD, LET US NOT LIVE IN FRANCE; LET US QUIT ALL AND GIVE OUR VINEYARDS TO A BARBAROUS PEOPLE.
O DIEU VIVANT! SHALL A FEW SPRAYS OF US, THE EMPTYING OF OUR FATHERS' LUXURY, OUR SCIONS PUT IN WILD AND SAVAGE STOCK, SPIRT UP SO SUDDENLY INTO THE CLOUDS, AND OVERLOOK THEIR GRAFTERS?

NORMANS, BUT BASTARD NORMANS, NORMAN BASTARDS! MORT DE MA VIE! IF THEY MARCH ALONG UNFOUGHT WITHAL, BUT I WILL SELL MY DUKEDOM, TO BUY A SLOBBERY AND A DIRTY FARM IN THAT NOOK-SHOTTEN ISLE OF ALBION.
DIEU DE BATAILLES! WHERE HAVE THEY THIS METTLE? IS NOT THEIR CLIMATE FOGGY, RAW AND DULL, ON WHOM, AS IN DESPITE, THE SUN LOOKS PALE, KILLING THEIR FRUIT WITH FROWNS?
CAN SODDEN WATER, A DRENCH FOR SUR-REIN'D JADES, THEIR BARLEY-BROTH, DECOCT THEIR COLD BLOOD TO SUCH VALIANT HEAT?

AND SHALL OUR QUICK BLOOD, SPIRITED WITH WINE, SEEM FROSTY? O, FOR HONOUR OF OUR LAND, LET US NOT HANG LIKE ROPING ICICLES UPON OUR HOUSES' THATCH, WHILES A MORE FROSTY PEOPLE SWEAT DROPS OF GALLANT YOUTH IN OUR RICH FIELDS! POOR WE MAY CALL THEM IN THEIR NATIVE LORDS.
BY FAITH AND HONOUR, OUR MADAMS MOCK AT US, AND PLAINLY SAY OUR METTLE IS BRED OUT, AND THEY WILL GIVE THEIR BODIES TO THE LUST OF ENGLISH YOUTH TO NEW-STORE FRANCE WITH BASTARD WARRIORS.
THEY BID US TO THE ENGLISH DANCING-SCHOOLS, AND TEACH LAVOLTAS HIGH, AND SWIFT CORANTOS; SAYING OUR GRACE IS ONLY IN OUR HEELS, AND THAT WE ARE MOST LOFTY RUNAWAYS.
WHERE IS MONTJOY THE HERALD? SPEED HIM HENCE: LET HIM GREET ENGLAND WITH OUR SHARP DEFIANCE.
UP, PRINCES! AND, WITH SPIRIT OF HONOUR EDG'D MORE SHARPER THAN YOUR SWORDS, HIE TO THE FIELD:
CHARLES DELABRETH, HIGH CONSTABLE OF FRANCE; YOU DUKES OF ORLEANS, BOURBON, AND OF BERRY, ALENÇON, BRABANT, BAR, AND BURGUNDY; JAQUES CHATILLON, RAMBURES, VAUDEMONT, BEAUMONT, GRANDPRÉ, ROUSSI, AND FAUCONBERG, FOIX, LESTRALE, BOUCIQUALT, AND CHAROLOIS;
HIGH DUKES, GREAT PRINCES, BARONS, LORDS, AND KNIGHTS, FOR YOUR GREAT SEATS NOW QUIT YOU OF GREAT SHAMES.

BAR HARRY ENGLAND, THAT SWEEPS THROUGH OUR LAND WITH PENNONS PAINTED IN THE BLOOD OF HARFLEUR. RUSH ON HIS HOST, AS DOTH THE MELTED SNOW UPON THE VALLEYS, WHOSE LOW VASSAL SEAT THE ALPS DOTH SPIT AND VOID HIS RHEUM UPON.
GO DOWN UPON HIM, -- YOU HAVE POWER ENOUGH, -- AND IN A CAPTIVE CHARIOT INTO ROUEN BRING HIM OUR PRISONER.
THIS BECOMES THE GREAT. SORRY AM I HIS NUMBERS ARE SO FEW, HIS SOLDIERS SICK, AND FAMISH'D IN THEIR MARCH;
FOR I AM SURE, WHEN HE SHALL SEE OUR ARMY, HE'LL DROP HIS HEART INTO THE SINK OF FEAR AND FOR ACHIEVEMENT OFFER US HIS RANSOM.
THEREFORE, LORD CONSTABLE, HASTE ON MONTJOY, AND LET HIM SAY TO ENGLAND THAT WE SEND TO KNOW WHAT WILLING RANSOM HE WILL GIVE. -- PRINCE DAUPHIN, YOU SHALL STAY WITH US IN ROUEN.
NOT SO, I DO BESEECH YOUR MAJESTY.
BE PATIENT, FOR YOU SHALL REMAIN WITH US.
NOW FORTH, LORD CONSTABLE AND PRINCES ALL, AND QUICKLY BRING US WORD OF ENGLAND'S FALL.

Act Three
Scene Six
FRANCE - THE ENGLISH CAMP OF PICARDY - 23RD OCTOBER 1415. NEAR THE BRIDGE OVER THE RIVER TERNOISE...
HOW NOW, CAPTAIN FLUELLEN! COME YOU FROM THE BRIDGE?
I ASSURE YOU, THERE IS VERY EXCELLENT SERVICES COMMITTED AT THE PRIDGE.
IS THE DUKE OF EXETER SAFE?

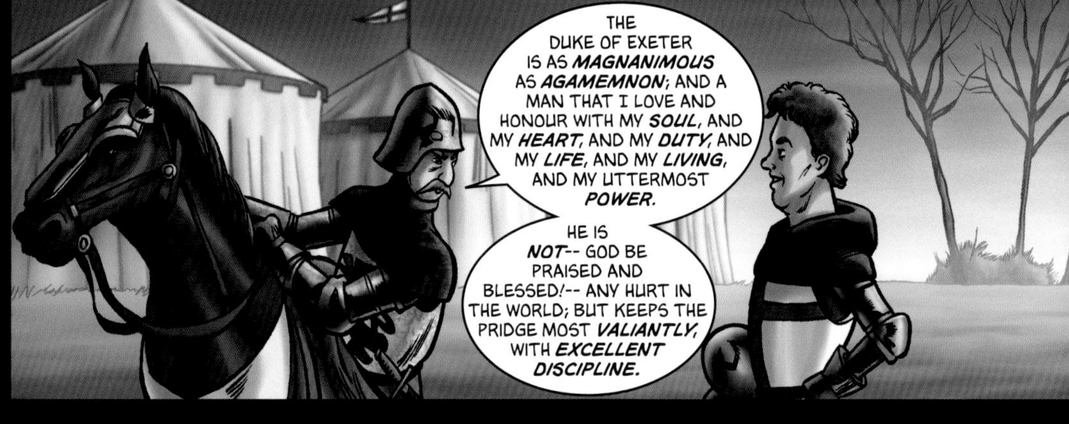
THE DUKE OF EXETER IS AS MAGNANIMOUS AS AGAMEMNON; AND A MAN THAT I LOVE AND HONOUR WITH MY SOUL, AND MY HEART, AND MY DUTY, AND MY LIFE, AND MY LIVING, AND MY UTTERMOST POWER.
HE IS NOT-- GOD BE PRAISED AND BLESSED!-- ANY HURT IN THE WORLD; BUT KEEPS THE PRIDGE MOST VALIANTLY, WITH EXCELLENT DISCIPLINE.

THERE IS AN AUNCHIENT LIEUTENANT THERE AT THE PRIDGE, I THINK IN MY VERY CONSCIENCE, HE IS AS VALIANT A MAN AS MARK ANTONY; AND HE IS A MAN OF NO ESTIMATION IN THE WORLD: BUT I DID SEE HIM DO AS GALLANT SERVICE.
WHAT DO YOU CALL HIM?
HE IS CALL'D AUNCHIENT PISTOL.
I KNOW HIM NOT.

HERE IS THE MAN.
CAPTAIN, I THEE BESEECH TO DO ME FAVOURS: THE DUKE OF EXETER DOTH LOVE THEE WELL.
AY, I PRAISE GOD; AND I HAVE MERITED SOME LOVE AT HIS HANDS.

BARDOLPH, A SOLDIER, FIRM AND SOUND OF HEART, AND OF BUXOM VALOUR, HATH BY CRUEL FATE AND GIDDY FORTUNE'S FURIOUS FICKLE WHEEL, THAT GODDESS BLIND, THAT STANDS UPON THE ROLLING RESTLESS STONE--
BY YOUR PATIENCE, AUNCHIENT PISTOL. FORTUNE IS PAINTED BLIND, WITH A MUFFLER AFORE HER EYES, TO SIGNIFY TO YOU THAT FORTUNE IS BLIND; AND SHE IS PAINTED ALSO WITH A WHEEL, TO SIGNIFY TO YOU, WHICH IS THE MORAL OF IT, THAT SHE IS TURNING, AND INCONSTANT, AND MUTABILITY, AND VARIATION;
AND HER FOOT, LOOK YOU, IS FIXED UPON A SPHERICAL STONE, WHICH ROLLS, AND ROLLS, AND ROLLS. IN GOOD TRUTH, THE POET MAKES A MOST EXCELLENT DESCRIPTION OF IT: FORTUNE IS AN EXCELLENT MORAL.
FORTUNE IS BARDOLPH'S FOE, AND FROWNS ON HIM; FOR HE HATH STOLEN A PAX, AND HANGED MUST 'A BE,-- A DAMNED DEATH!
LET GALLOWS GAPE FOR DOG; LET MAN GO FREE, AND LET NOT HEMP HIS WINDPIPE SUFFOCATE. BUT EXETER HATH GIVEN THE DOOM OF DEATH FOR PAX OF LITTLE PRICE.

THEREFORE, GO SPEAK-- THE DUKE WILL HEAR THY VOICE-- AND LET NOT BARDOLPH'S VITAL THREAD BE CUT WITH EDGE OF PENNY CORD AND VILE REPROACH. SPEAK, CAPTAIN, FOR HIS LIFE, AND I WILL THEE REQUITE.
AUNCHIENT PISTOL, I DO PARTLY UNDER-STAND YOUR MEANING.

WHY THEN, REJOICE THEREFORE.
CERTAINLY, AUNCHIENT, IT IS NOT A THING TO REJOICE AT; FOR IF, LOOK YOU, HE WERE MY BROTHER, I WOULD DESIRE THE DUKE TO USE HIS GOOD PLEASURE, AND PUT HIM TO EXECUTION; FOR DISCIPLINE OUGHT TO BE USED.

DIE AND BE DAMN'D! AND FIGO FOR THY FRIENDSHIP!
IT IS WELL.

THE FIG OF SPAIN!
VERY GOOD.
WHY, THIS IS AN ARRANT COUNTERFEIT RASCAL. I REMEMBER HIM NOW; A BAWD, A CUTPURSE.

I'LL ASSURE YOU, 'A UTTERED AS PRAVE WORDS AT THE PRIDGE AS YOU SHALL SEE IN A SUMMER'S DAY. BUT IT IS VERY WELL; WHAT HE HAS SPOKE TO ME, THAT IS WELL, I WARRANT YOU, WHEN TIME IS SERVE.
WHY, 'TIS A GULL, A FOOL, A ROGUE, THAT NOW AND THEN GOES TO THE WARS, TO GRACE HIMSELF AT HIS RETURN INTO LONDON UNDER THE FORM OF A SOLDIER.

AND SUCH FELLOWS ARE PERFECT IN THE GREAT COMMANDERS' NAMES; AND THEY WILL LEARN YOU BY ROTE WHERE SERVICES WERE DONE; AT SUCH AND SUCH A SCONCE, AT SUCH A BREACH, AT SUCH A CONVOY; WHO CAME OFF BRAVELY, WHO WAS SHOT, WHO DISGRAC'D, WHAT TERMS THE ENEMY STOOD ON;
AND THIS THEY CON PERFECTLY IN THE PHRASE OF WAR, WHICH THEY TRICK UP WITH NEW-TUNED OATHS: AND WHAT A BEARD OF THE GENERAL'S CUT AND A HORRID SUIT OF THE CAMP WILL DO AMONG FOAMING BOTTLES AND ALE-WASH'D WITS, IS WONDERFUL TO BE THOUGHT ON.

BUT YOU MUST LEARN TO KNOW SUCH SLANDERS OF THE AGE, OR ELSE YOU MAY BE MARVELLOUSLY MISTOOK.
I TELL YOU WHAT, CAPTAIN GOWER; I DO PERCEIVE HE IS NOT THE MAN THAT HE WOULD GLADLY MAKE SHOW TO THE WORLD HE IS. IF I FIND A HOLE IN HIS COAT, I WILL TELL HIM MY MIND.
B-DUM B-DUM
HARK YOU, THE KING IS COMING, AND I MUST SPEAK WITH HIM FROM THE PRIDGE.
GOD PLESS YOUR MAJESTY!
HOW NOW, FLUELLEN? CAM'ST THOU FROM THE BRIDGE?
AY, SO PLEASE YOUR MAJESTY. THE DUKE OF EXETER HAS VERY GALLANTLY MAINTAIN'D THE PRIDGE. THE FRENCH IS GONE OFF, LOOK YOU; AND THERE IS GALLANT AND MOST PRAVE PASSAGES.
MARRY, TH'ATHVERSARY WAS HAVE POSSESSION OF THE PRIDGE; BUT HE IS ENFORCED TO RETIRE, AND THE DUKE OF EXETER IS MASTER OF THE PRIDGE:
I CAN TELL YOUR MAJESTY, THE DUKE IS A PRAVE MAN.

WHAT MEN HAVE YOU LOST, FLUELLEN?
THE PERDITION OF TH'ATHVERSARY HATH BEEN VERY GREAT, REASONABLE GREAT: MARRY, FOR MY PART, I THINK THE DUKE HATH LOST NEVER A MAN, BUT ONE THAT IS LIKE TO BE EXECUTED FOR ROBBING A CHURCH, ONE BARDOLPH, IF YOUR MAJESTY KNOW THE MAN:
HIS FACE IS ALL BUBUKLES, AND WHELKS, AND KNOBS, AND FLAMES O' FIRE; AND HIS LIPS BLOWS AT HIS NOSE, AND IT IS LIKE A COAL OF FIRE, SOMETIMES PLUE AND SOMETIMES RED;
BUT HIS NOSE IS EXECUTED AND HIS FIRE'S OUT.
WE WOULD HAVE ALL SUCH OFFENDERS SO CUT OFF; AND WE GIVE EXPRESS CHARGE, THAT IN OUR MARCHES THROUGH THE COUNTRY, THERE BE NOTHING COMPELLED FROM THE VILLAGES, NOTHING TAKEN BUT PAID FOR, NONE OF THE FRENCH UPBRAIDED OR ABUSED IN DISDAINFUL LANGUAGE;
FOR WHEN LENITY AND CRUELTY PLAY FOR A KINGDOM, THE GENTLER GAMESTER IS THE SOONEST WINNER.

TAN-TARA!
YOU KNOW ME BY MY HABIT.
MY MASTER'S MIND.
WELL THEN I KNOW THEE. WHAT SHALL I KNOW OF THEE?
UNFOLD IT.

THUS SAYS MY KING:-- SAY THOU TO HARRY OF ENGLAND:
THOUGH WE SEEM'D DEAD, WE DID BUT SLEEP; ADVANTAGE IS A BETTER SOLDIER THAN RASHNESS. TELL HIM WE COULD HAVE REBUK'D HIM AT HARFLEUR, BUT THAT WE THOUGHT NOT GOOD TO BRUISE AN INJURY TILL IT WERE FULL RIPE. NOW WE SPEAK UPON OUR CUE, AND OUR VOICE IS IMPERIAL.
ENGLAND SHALL REPENT HIS FOLLY, SEE HIS WEAKNESS, AND ADMIRE OUR SUFFERANCE. BID HIM, THEREFORE, CONSIDER OF HIS RANSOM; WHICH MUST PROPORTION THE LOSSES WE HAVE BORNE, THE SUBJECTS WE HAVE LOST, THE DISGRACE WE HAVE DIGESTED; WHICH IN WEIGHT TO RE-ANSWER, HIS PETTINESS WOULD BOW UNDER.

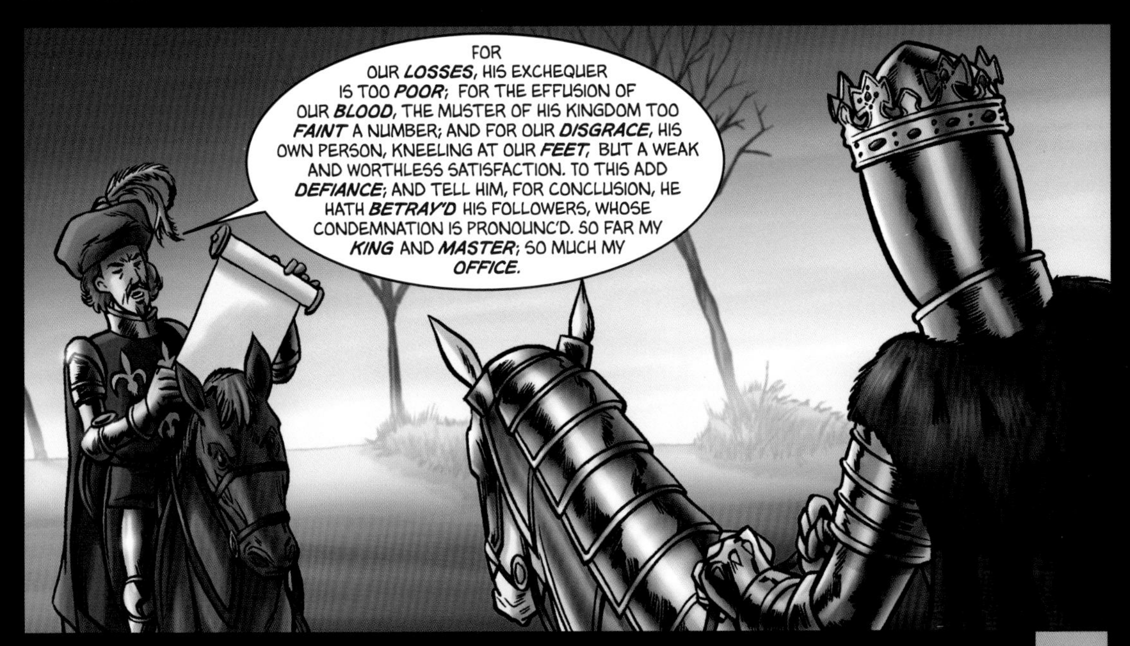
FOR OUR LOSSES, HIS EXCHEQUER IS TOO POOR; FOR THE EFFUSION OF OUR BLOOD, THE MUSTER OF HIS KINGDOM TOO FAINT A NUMBER; AND FOR OUR DISGRACE, HIS OWN PERSON, KNEELING AT OUR FEET, BUT A WEAK AND WORTHLESS SATISFACTION. TO THIS ADD DEFIANCE; AND TELL HIM, FOR CONCLUSION, HE HATH BETRAY'D HIS FOLLOWERS, WHOSE CONDEMNATION IS PRONOUNC'D. SO FAR MY KING AND MASTER; SO MUCH MY OFFICE.

WHAT IS THY NAME? I KNOW THY QUALITY.
MONTJOY.
THOU DOST THY OFFICE FAIRLY.
TURN THEE BACK. AND TELL THY KING, -- I DO NOT SEEK HIM NOW, BUT COULD BE WILLING TO MARCH ON TO CALAIS WITHOUT IMPEACHMENT;
FOR, TO SAY THE SOOTH, THOUGH 'TIS NO WISDOM TO CONFESS SO MUCH UNTO AN ENEMY OF CRAFT AND VANTAGE, MY PEOPLE ARE WITH SICKNESS MUCH ENFEEBLED, MY NUMBERS LESSEN'D, AND THOSE FEW I HAVE ALMOST NO BETTER THAN SO MANY FRENCH; WHO WHEN THEY WERE IN HEALTH, I TELL THEE, HERALD, I THOUGHT UPON ONE PAIR OF ENGLISH LEGS DID MARCH THREE FRENCHMEN.
YET, FORGIVE ME, GOD, THAT I DO BRAG THUS! -- THIS YOUR AIR OF FRANCE HATH BLOWN THAT VICE IN ME. I MUST REPENT.
GO THEREFORE, TELL THY MASTER HERE I AM; MY RANSOM IS THIS FRAIL AND WORTHLESS TRUNK, MY ARMY BUT A WEAK AND SICKLY GUARD; YET, GOD BEFORE, TELL HIM WE WILL COME ON, THOUGH FRANCE HIMSELF AND SUCH ANOTHER NEIGHBOUR STAND IN OUR WAY.
THERE'S FOR THY LABOUR, MONTJOY.
GO, BID THY MASTER WELL ADVISE HIMSELF. IF WE MAY PASS, WE WILL; IF WE BE HINDER'D, WE SHALL YOUR TAWNY GROUND WITH YOUR RED BLOOD DISCOLOUR; AND SO, MONTJOY, FARE YOU WELL. THE SUM OF ALL OUR ANSWER IS BUT THIS:
WE WOULD NOT SEEK A BATTLE, AS WE ARE; NOR, AS WE ARE, WE SAY, WE WILL NOT SHUN IT. SO TELL YOUR MASTER.
I SHALL DELIVER SO. THANKS TO YOUR HIGHNESS.
I HOPE THEY WILL NOT COME UPON US NOW.
WE ARE IN GOD'S HAND, BROTHER, NOT IN THEIRS.
MARCH TO THE BRIDGE; IT NOW DRAWS TOWARD NIGHT. BEYOND THE RIVER WE'LL ENCAMP OURSELVES, AND ON TO-MORROW, BID THEM MARCH AWAY.

Act Three
Scene Seven
THE FRENCH CAMP, AGINCOURT - 24TH OCTOBER 1415. THE NIGHT BEFORE THE BATTLE...
TUT! I HAVE THE BEST ARMOUR OF THE WORLD.
WOULD IT WERE DAY!
YOU HAVE AN EXCELLENT ARMOUR; BUT LET MY HORSE HAVE HIS DUE.
IT IS THE BEST HORSE OF EUROPE.
WILL IT NEVER BE MORNING?
MY LORD OF ORLEANS, AND MY LORD HIGH CONSTABLE, YOU TALK OF HORSE AND ARMOUR?

YOU ARE AS WELL PROVIDED OF BOTH AS ANY PRINCE IN THE WORLD.
WHAT A LONG NIGHT IS THIS! I WILL NOT CHANGE MY HORSE WITH ANY THAT TREADS BUT ON FOUR PASTERNS. ÇA, HA! HE BOUNDS FROM THE EARTH, AS IF HIS ENTRAILS WERE HAIRS; LE CHEVAL VOLANT, THE PEGASUS, QUI A LES NARINES DE FEU!
WHEN I BESTRIDE HIM, I SOAR, I AM A HAWK. HE TROTS THE AIR; THE EARTH SINGS WHEN HE TOUCHES IT; THE BASEST HORN OF HIS HOOF IS MORE MUSICAL THAN THE PIPE OF HERMES.
HE'S OF THE COLOUR OF THE NUTMEG.
AND OF THE HEAT OF THE GINGER. IT IS A BEAST FOR PERSEUS. HE IS PURE AIR AND FIRE; AND THE DULL ELEMENTS OF EARTH AND WATER NEVER APPEAR IN HIM, BUT ONLY IN PATIENT STILLNESS WHILE HIS RIDER MOUNTS HIM.
HE IS INDEED A HORSE, AND ALL OTHER JADES YOU MAY CALL BEASTS.
INDEED, MY LORD, IT IS A MOST ABSOLUTE AND EXCELLENT HORSE.
IT IS THE PRINCE OF PALFREYS; HIS NEIGH IS LIKE THE BIDDING OF A MONARCH, AND HIS COUNTENANCE ENFORCES HOMAGE.
NO MORE, COUSIN.
NAY, THE MAN HATH NO WIT THAT CANNOT, FROM THE RISING OF THE LARK TO THE LODGING OF THE LAMB, VARY DESERVED PRAISE ON MY PALFREY. IT IS A THEME AS FLUENT AS THE SEA; TURN THE SANDS INTO ELOQUENT TONGUES, AND MY HORSE IS ARGUMENT FOR THEM ALL:
'TIS A SUBJECT FOR A SOVEREIGN TO REASON ON, AND FOR A SOVEREIGN'S SOVEREIGN TO RIDE ON; AND FOR THE WORLD, FAMILIAR TO US AND UNKNOWN, TO LAY APART THEIR PARTICULAR FUNCTIONS AND WONDER AT HIM.
I ONCE WRIT A SONNET IN HIS PRAISE AND BEGAN THUS: "WONDER OF NATURE,"...

I HAVE HEARD A SONNET BEGIN SO TO ONE'S MISTRESS.
THEN DID THEY IMITATE THAT WHICH I COMPOS'D TO MY COURSER, FOR MY HORSE IS MY MISTRESS.
YOUR MISTRESS BEARS WELL.
ME WELL; WHICH IS THE PRESCRIPT PRAISE AND PERFECTION OF A GOOD AND PARTICULAR MISTRESS.
NAY, FOR METHOUGHT YESTERDAY, YOUR MISTRESS SHREWDLY SHOOK YOUR BACK.
SO PERHAPS, DID YOURS.
MINE WAS NOT BRIDLED.
O! THEN, BELIKE, SHE WAS OLD AND GENTLE; AND YOU RODE, LIKE A KERN OF IRELAND, YOUR FRENCH HOSE OFF, AND IN YOUR STRAIT STROSSERS.
YOU HAVE GOOD JUDGMENT IN HORSEMAN-SHIP.
BE WARN'D BY ME, THEN; THEY THAT RIDE SO AND RIDE NOT WARILY, FALL INTO FOUL BOGS. I HAD RATHER HAVE MY HORSE TO MY MISTRESS.
I HAD AS LIEF HAVE MY MISTRESS A JADE.
I TELL THEE, CONSTABLE, MY MISTRESS WEARS HIS OWN HAIR.
I COULD MAKE AS TRUE A BOAST AS THAT, IF I HAD A SOW TO MY MISTRESS.
"LE CHIEN EST RETOURNÉ À SON PROPRE VOMISSEMENT, ET LA TRUIE LAVÉE AU BOURBIER;" THOU MAKEST USE OF ANY THING.
YET DO I NOT USE MY HORSE FOR MY MISTRESS, OR ANY SUCH PROVERB SO LITTLE KIN TO THE PURPOSE.
MY LORD CONSTABLE, THE ARMOUR THAT I SAW IN YOUR TENT TO-NIGHT, ARE THOSE STARS OR SUNS UPON IT?
STARS, MY LORD.
SOME OF THEM WILL FALL TO-MORROW, I HOPE.

AND YET MY SKY SHALL NOT WANT.
THAT MAY BE, FOR YOU BEAR A MANY SUPERFLUOUSLY, AND 'TWERE MORE HONOUR SOME WERE AWAY.
EVEN AS YOUR HORSE BEARS YOUR PRAISES, WHO WOULD TROT AS WELL, WERE SOME OF YOUR BRAGS DISMOUNTED.
WOULD I WERE ABLE TO LOAD HIM WITH HIS DESERT!
WILL IT NEVER BE DAY?
I WILL TROT TO-MORROW A MILE, AND MY WAY SHALL BE PAVED WITH ENGLISH FACES.
I WILL NOT SAY SO, FOR FEAR I SHOULD BE FAC'D OUT OF MY WAY. BUT I WOULD IT WERE MORNING; FOR I WOULD FAIN BE ABOUT THE EARS OF THE ENGLISH.
WHO WILL GO TO HAZARD WITH ME FOR TWENTY PRISONERS?
YOU MUST FIRST GO YOURSELF TO HAZARD, ERE YOU HAVE THEM.
'TIS MIDNIGHT; I'LL GO ARM MYSELF.

THE DAUPHIN LONGS FOR MORNING.
HE LONGS TO EAT THE ENGLISH.
I THINK HE WILL EAT ALL HE KILLS.
BY THE WHITE HAND OF MY LADY, HE'S A GALLANT PRINCE.
SWEAR BY HER FOOT, THAT SHE MAY TREAD OUT THE OATH.
HE IS SIMPLY THE MOST ACTIVE GENTLEMAN OF FRANCE.
DOING IS ACTIVITY; AND HE WILL STILL BE DOING.
HE NEVER DID HARM, THAT I HEARD OF.
NOR WILL DO NONE TO-MORROW: HE WILL KEEP THAT GOOD NAME STILL.
I KNOW HIM TO BE VALIANT.
I WAS TOLD THAT BY ONE THAT KNOWS HIM BETTER THAN YOU.
WHAT'S HE?
MARRY, HE TOLD ME SO HIMSELF; AND HE SAID HE CAR'D NOT WHO KNEW IT.
HE NEEDS NOT; IT IS NO HIDDEN VIRTUE IN HIM.
BY MY FAITH, SIR, BUT IT IS; NEVER ANYBODY SAW IT BUT HIS LACKEY. 'TIS A HOODED VALOUR; AND WHEN IT APPEARS, IT WILL BATE.

"ILL WILL NEVER SAID WELL."
I WILL CAP THAT PROVERB WITH "THERE IS FLATTERY IN FRIENDSHIP."
AND I WILL TAKE UP THAT WITH "GIVE THE DEVIL HIS DUE."
WELL PLAC'D: THERE STANDS YOUR FRIEND FOR THE DEVIL; HAVE AT THE VERY EYE OF THAT PROVERB WITH "A POX OF THE DEVIL."
YOU ARE THE BETTER AT PROVERBS, BY HOW MUCH "A FOOL'S BOLT IS SOON SHOT."
YOU HAVE SHOT OVER.
'TIS NOT THE FIRST TIME YOU WERE OVERSHOT.
MY LORD HIGH CONSTABLE, THE ENGLISH LIE WITHIN FIFTEEN HUNDRED PACES OF YOUR TENTS.
WHO HATH MEASUR'D THE GROUND?
THE LORD GRANDPRÉ.
A VALIANT AND MOST EXPERT GENTLEMAN.
WOULD IT WERE DAY! -- ALAS, POOR HARRY OF ENGLAND! -- HE LONGS NOT FOR THE DAWNING, AS WE DO.
WHAT A WRETCHED AND PEEVISH FELLOW IS THIS KING OF ENGLAND, TO MOPE WITH HIS FAT-BRAIN'D FOLLOWERS SO FAR OUT OF HIS KNOWLEDGE!

IF THE ENGLISH HAD ANY APPREHENSION, THEY WOULD RUN AWAY.
THAT THEY LACK; FOR IF THEIR HEADS HAD ANY INTELLECTUAL ARMOUR, THEY COULD NEVER WEAR SUCH HEAVY HEAD-PIECES.
THAT ISLAND OF ENGLAND BREEDS VERY VALIANT CREATURES. THEIR MASTIFFS ARE OF UNMATCHABLE COURAGE.
FOOLISH CURS, THAT RUN WINKING INTO THE MOUTH OF A RUSSIAN BEAR AND HAVE THEIR HEADS CRUSH'D LIKE ROTTEN APPLES! YOU MAY AS WELL SAY, THAT'S A VALIANT FLEA THAT DARE EAT HIS BREAKFAST ON THE LIP OF A LION.
JUST, JUST; AND THE MEN DO SYMPATHIZE WITH THE MASTIFFS IN ROBUSTIOUS AND ROUGH COMING ON, LEAVING THEIR WITS WITH THEIR WIVES; AND THEN, GIVE THEM GREAT MEALS OF BEEF, AND IRON AND STEEL, THEY WILL EAT LIKE WOLVES AND FIGHT LIKE DEVILS.
AY, BUT THESE ENGLISH ARE SHREWDLY OUT OF BEEF.
THEN SHALL WE FIND TO-MORROW THEY HAVE ONLY STOMACHS TO EAT AND NONE TO FIGHT. NOW IS IT TIME TO ARM; COME, SHALL WE ABOUT IT?
IT IS NOW TWO O'CLOCK; BUT, LET ME SEE, BY TEN WE SHALL HAVE EACH A HUNDRED ENGLISHMEN.

Act Four
Prologue
NOW ENTERTAIN CONJECTURE OF A TIME, WHEN CREEPING MURMUR, AND THE PORING DARK, FILLS THE WIDE VESSEL OF THE UNIVERSE.
FROM CAMP TO CAMP, THROUGH THE FOUL WOMB OF NIGHT, THE HUM OF EITHER ARMY STILLY SOUNDS, THAT THE FIX'D SENTINELS ALMOST RECEIVE THE SECRET WHISPERS OF EACH OTHER'S WATCH;

FIRE ANSWERS FIRE, AND THROUGH THEIR PALY FLAMES EACH BATTLE SEES THE OTHER'S UMBER'D FACE;
STEED THREATENS STEED, IN HIGH AND BOASTFUL NEIGHS PIERCING THE NIGHT'S DULL EAR; AND FROM THE TENTS, THE ARMOURERS, ACCOMPLISHING THE KNIGHTS, WITH BUSY HAMMERS CLOSING RIVETS UP, GIVE DREADFUL NOTE OF PREPARATION.

THE COUNTRY COCKS DO CROW, THE CLOCKS DO TOLL, AND THE THIRD HOUR OF DROWSY MORNING NAME.
PROUD OF THEIR NUMBERS, AND SECURE IN SOUL, THE CONFIDENT AND OVER-LUSTY FRENCH DO THE LOW-RATED ENGLISH PLAY AT DICE; AND CHIDE THE CRIPPLE TARDY-GAITED NIGHT, WHO, LIKE A FOUL AND UGLY WITCH, DOTH LIMP SO TEDIOUSLY AWAY.
THE POOR CONDEMNED ENGLISH, LIKE SACRIFICES, BY THEIR WATCHFUL FIRES SIT PATIENTLY AND INLY RUMINATE THE MORNING'S DANGER; AND THEIR GESTURE SAD, INVESTING LANK-LEAN CHEEKS AND WAR-WORN COATS, PRESENTETH THEM UNTO THE GAZING MOON SO MANY HORRID GHOSTS. -- O! NOW, WHO WILL BEHOLD THE ROYAL CAPTAIN OF THIS RUIN'D BAND WALKING FROM WATCH TO WATCH, FROM TENT TO TENT, LET HIM CRY "PRAISE AND GLORY ON HIS HEAD!"
FOR FORTH HE GOES AND VISITS ALL HIS HOST, BIDS THEM GOOD MORROW WITH A MODEST SMILE, AND CALLS THEM BROTHERS, FRIENDS, AND COUNTRYMEN.
UPON HIS ROYAL FACE THERE IS NO NOTE HOW DREAD AN ARMY HATH ENROUNDED HIM; NOR DOTH HE DEDICATE ONE JOT OF COLOUR UNTO THE WEARY AND ALL-WATCHED NIGHT, BUT FRESHLY LOOKS, AND OVER-BEARS ATTAINT WITH CHEERFUL SEMBLANCE AND SWEET MAJESTY; THAT EVERY WRETCH, PINING AND PALE BEFORE, BEHOLDING HIM, PLUCKS COMFORT FROM HIS LOOKS.
A LARGESS UNIVERSAL, LIKE THE SUN, HIS LIBERAL EYE DOTH GIVE TO EVERY ONE, THAWING COLD FEAR, THAT MEAN AND GENTLE ALL BEHOLD, AS MAY UNWORTHINESS DEFINE,
A LITTLE TOUCH OF HARRY IN THE NIGHT.
AND SO OUR SCENE MUST TO THE BATTLE FLY; WHERE -- O FOR PITY! -- WE SHALL MUCH DISGRACE WITH FOUR OR FIVE MOST VILE AND RAGGED FOILS, RIGHT ILL-DISPOS'D IN BRAWL RIDICULOUS, THE NAME OF AGINCOURT.
YET, SIT AND SEE; MINDING TRUE THINGS BY WHAT THEIR MOCKERIES BE.

Act Four
Scene One
THE ENGLISH CAMP, AGINCOURT - 25TH OCTOBER 1415. THE EARLY MORNING BEFORE THE BATTLE...
GLOUCESTER, 'TIS TRUE THAT WE ARE IN GREAT DANGER; THE GREATER THEREFORE SHOULD OUR COURAGE BE.
GOOD MORROW, BROTHER BEDFORD.
GOD ALMIGHTY! THERE IS SOME SOUL OF GOODNESS IN THINGS EVIL, WOULD MEN OBSERVINGLY DISTIL IT OUT;
FOR OUR BAD NEIGHBOUR MAKES US EARLY STIRRERS, WHICH IS BOTH HEALTHFUL AND GOOD HUSBANDRY. BESIDES, THEY ARE OUR OUTWARD CONSCIENCES, AND PREACHERS TO US ALL; ADMONISHING, THAT WE SHOULD DRESS US FAIRLY FOR OUR END.
THUS MAY WE GATHER HONEY FROM THE WEED, AND MAKE A MORAL OF THE DEVIL HIMSELF.
GOOD MORROW, OLD SIR THOMAS ERPINGHAM: A GOOD SOFT PILLOW FOR THAT GOOD WHITE HEAD WERE BETTER THAN A CHURLISH TURF OF FRANCE.
NOT SO, MY LIEGE; THIS LODGING LIKES ME BETTER, SINCE I MAY SAY, "NOW LIE I LIKE A KING."
'TIS GOOD FOR MEN TO LOVE THEIR PRESENT PAINS UPON EXAMPLE; SO THE SPIRIT IS EASED;
AND WHEN THE MIND IS QUICKEN'D, OUT OF DOUBT, THE ORGANS, THOUGH DEFUNCT AND DEAD BEFORE, BREAK UP THEIR DROWSY GRAVE, AND NEWLY MOVE WITH CASTED SLOUGH AND FRESH LEGERITY.

LEND ME THY CLOAK, SIR THOMAS.
BROTHERS BOTH, COMMEND ME TO THE PRINCES IN OUR CAMP; DO MY GOOD MORROW TO THEM; AND ANON, DESIRE THEM ALL TO MY PAVILION.
WE SHALL, MY LIEGE.
SHALL I ATTEND YOUR GRACE?
NO, MY GOOD KNIGHT; GO WITH MY BROTHERS TO MY LORDS OF ENGLAND. I AND MY BOSOM MUST DEBATE AWHILE, AND THEN I WOULD NO OTHER COMPANY.
THE LORD IN HEAVEN BLESS THEE, NOBLE HARRY!
GOD-A-MERCY, OLD HEART! THOU SPEAK'ST CHEERFULLY.
QUI VA LĂ?
A FRIEND.
DISCUSS UNTO ME; ART THOU OFFICER? OR ART THOU BASE, COMMON, AND POPULAR?
I AM A GENTLEMAN OF A COMPANY.
TRAIL'ST THOU THE PUISSANT PIKE?
EVEN SO. WHAT ARE YOU?

AS GOOD A GENTLEMAN AS THE EMPEROR.
THEN YOU ARE A BETTER THAN THE KING.
THE KING'S A BAWCOCK, AND A HEART OF GOLD, A LAD OF LIFE, AN IMP OF FAME; OF PARENTS GOOD, OF FIST MOST VALIANT.
I KISS HIS DIRTY SHOE, AND FROM HEART-STRING I LOVE THE LOVELY BULLY. WHAT IS THY NAME?
HARRY LE ROY.
LE ROY! A CORNISH NAME. ART THOU OF CORNISH CREW?
NO, I AM A WELSHMAN.
KNOW'ST THOU FLUELLEN?
YES.
TELL HIM, I'LL KNOCK HIS LEEK ABOUT HIS PATE UPON SAINT DAVY'S DAY.
DO NOT YOU WEAR YOUR DAGGER IN YOUR CAP THAT DAY, LEST HE KNOCK THAT ABOUT YOURS.
ART THOU HIS FRIEND?
AND HIS KINSMAN TOO.
THE FIGO FOR THEE, THEN!
I THANK YOU.
GOD BE WITH YOU!
MY NAME IS PISTOL CALLED.
IT SORTS WELL WITH YOUR FIERCENESS.

CAPTAIN FLUELLEN!
SO! IN THE NAME OF JESU CHRIST, SPEAK LOWER. IT IS THE GREATEST ADMIRATION IN THE UNIVERSAL WORLD, WHEN THE TRUE AND AUNCHIENT PREROGATIFES AND LAWS OF THE WARS IS NOT KEPT.
IF YOU WOULD TAKE THE PAINS BUT TO EXAMINE THE WARS OF POMPEY THE GREAT, YOU SHALL FIND, I WARRANT YOU, THAT THERE IS NO TIDDLE TADDLE, NOR PIBBLE PABBLE, IN POMPEY'S CAMP. I WARRANT YOU, YOU SHALL FIND THE CEREMONIES OF THE WARS, AND THE CARES OF IT, AND THE FORMS OF IT, AND THE SOBRIETY OF IT, AND THE MODESTY OF IT, TO BE OTHERWISE.
HA HA HA!!
HA HA HA!!
WHY, THE ENEMY IS LOUD; YOU HEAR HIM ALL NIGHT.
IF THE ENEMY IS AN ASS AND A FOOL, AND A PRATING COXCOMB, IS IT MEET, THINK YOU, THAT WE SHOULD ALSO, LOOK YOU, BE AN ASS AND A FOOL, AND A PRATING COXCOMB? IN YOUR OWN CONSCIENCE, NOW?
I WILL SPEAK LOWER.
I PRAY YOU, AND BESEECH YOU, THAT YOU WILL.
THOUGH IT APPEAR A LITTLE OUT OF FASHION, THERE IS MUCH CARE AND VALOUR IN THIS WELSHMAN.

BROTHER JOHN BATES, IS NOT THAT THE MORNING WHICH BREAKS YONDER?
I THINK IT BE; BUT WE HAVE NO GREAT CAUSE TO DESIRE THE APPROACH OF DAY.
WE SEE YONDER THE BEGINNING OF THE DAY, BUT I THINK WE SHALL NEVER SEE THE END OF IT.

WHO GOES THERE?
A FRIEND.
UNDER WHAT CAPTAIN SERVE YOU?
UNDER SIR THOMAS ERPINGHAM.
A GOOD OLD COMMANDER, AND A MOST KIND GENTLEMAN. I PRAY YOU, WHAT THINKS HE OF OUR ESTATE?
EVEN AS MEN WRECK'D UPON A SAND, THAT LOOK TO BE WASH'D OFF THE NEXT TIDE.
HE HATH NOT TOLD HIS THOUGHT TO THE KING?

NO; NOR IT IS NOT MEET HE SHOULD.
FOR, THOUGH I SPEAK IT TO YOU, I THINK THE KING IS BUT A MAN, AS I AM. THE VIOLET SMELLS TO HIM AS IT DOTH TO ME; THE ELEMENT SHOWS TO HIM, AS IT DOTH TO ME; ALL HIS SENSES HAVE BUT HUMAN CONDITIONS.
HIS CEREMONIES LAID BY, IN HIS NAKEDNESS HE APPEARS BUT A MAN; AND THOUGH HIS AFFECTIONS ARE HIGHER MOUNTED THAN OURS, YET, WHEN THEY STOOP, THEY STOOP WITH THE LIKE WING.
THEREFORE, WHEN HE SEES REASON OF FEARS, AS WE DO, HIS FEARS, OUT OF DOUBT, BE OF THE SAME RELISH AS OURS ARE; YET, IN REASON, NO MAN SHOULD POSSESS HIM WITH ANY APPEARANCE OF FEAR, LEST HE, BY SHOWING IT, SHOULD DISHEARTEN HIS ARMY.

HE MAY SHOW WHAT OUTWARD COURAGE HE WILL; BUT I BELIEVE, AS COLD A NIGHT AS 'TIS, HE COULD WISH HIMSELF IN *THAMES* UP TO THE NECK;
AND SO I WOULD HE *WERE,* AND I *BY* HIM, AT ALL ADVENTURES, SO WE WERE *QUIT* HERE.
BY MY TROTH, I WILL SPEAK MY *CONSCIENCE* OF THE KING: I THINK HE WOULD NOT WISH HIMSELF *ANYWHERE* BUT WHERE HE *IS.*
THEN I WOULD HE WERE HERE *ALONE;* SO SHOULD HE BE SURE TO BE *RANSOMED,* AND A MANY POOR MEN'S LIVES SAVED.
I DARE SAY, YOU LOVE HIM NOT SO ILL, TO WISH HIM HERE ALONE, *HOWSOEVER* YOU SPEAK THIS, TO FEEL OTHER MEN'S MINDS. METHINKS I COULD NOT DIE ANYWHERE SO *CONTENTED* AS IN THE *KING'S COMPANY,* HIS CAUSE BEING *JUST* AND HIS QUARREL *HONOURABLE.*
THAT'S MORE THAN WE KNOW.
AY, OR MORE THAN WE SHOULD SEEK AFTER; FOR WE KNOW ENOUGH, IF WE KNOW WE ARE THE *KING'S SUBJECTS.* IF HIS CAUSE BE *WRONG,* OUR OBEDIENCE TO THE KING WIPES THE CRIME OF IT *OUT* OF US.
BUT IF THE CAUSE BE *NOT* GOOD, THE KING HIMSELF HATH A HEAVY *RECKONING* TO MAKE, WHEN ALL THOSE LEGS AND ARMS AND HEADS, CHOPP'D OFF IN A BATTLE, SHALL JOIN TOGETHER AT THE LATTER DAY AND CRY ALL, *"WE DIED AT SUCH A PLACE";*
SOME *SWEARING,* SOME CRYING FOR A *SURGEON,* SOME UPON THEIR WIVES LEFT *POOR* BEHIND THEM, SOME UPON THE *DEBTS* THEY OWE, SOME UPON THEIR *CHILDREN* RAWLY LEFT.

I AM AFEARD THERE ARE FEW DIE WELL THAT DIE IN A BATTLE; FOR HOW CAN THEY CHARITABLY DISPOSE OF ANYTHING, WHEN BLOOD IS THEIR ARGUMENT? NOW, IF THESE MEN DO NOT DIE WELL, IT WILL BE A BLACK MATTER FOR THE KING THAT LED THEM TO IT; WHO TO DISOBEY WERE AGAINST ALL PROPORTION OF SUBJECTION.
SO, IF A SON THAT IS BY HIS FATHER SENT ABOUT MERCHANDISE DO SINFULLY MISCARRY UPON THE SEA, THE IMPUTATION OF HIS WICKEDNESS, BY YOUR RULE, SHOULD BE IMPOSED UPON HIS FATHER THAT SENT HIM;
OR IF A SERVANT, UNDER HIS MASTER'S COMMAND, TRANSPORTING A SUM OF MONEY, BE ASSAILED BY ROBBERS, AND DIE IN MANY IRRECONCIL'D INIQUITIES, YOU MAY CALL THE BUSINESS OF THE MASTER THE AUTHOR OF THE SERVANT'S DAMNATION.
BUT THIS IS NOT SO. THE KING IS NOT BOUND TO ANSWER THE PARTICULAR ENDINGS OF HIS SOLDIERS, THE FATHER OF HIS SON, NOR THE MASTER OF HIS SERVANT;
FOR THEY PURPOSE NOT THEIR DEATH, WHEN THEY PURPOSE THEIR SERVICES. BESIDES, THERE IS NO KING, BE HIS CAUSE NEVER SO SPOTLESS, IF IT COME TO THE ARBITREMENT OF SWORDS, CAN TRY IT OUT WITH ALL UNSPOTTED SOLDIERS.
SOME PERADVENTURE HAVE ON THEM THE GUILT OF PREMEDITATED AND CONTRIVED MURDER; SOME, OF BEGUILING VIRGINS WITH THE BROKEN SEALS OF PERJURY; SOME, MAKING THE WARS THEIR BULWARK, THAT HAVE BEFORE GORED THE GENTLE BOSOM OF PEACE WITH PILLAGE AND ROBBERY.
NOW, IF THESE MEN HAVE DEFEATED THE LAW AND OUTRUN NATIVE PUNISHMENT, THOUGH THEY CAN OUTSTRIP MEN, THEY HAVE NO WINGS TO FLY FROM GOD.

WAR IS HIS BEADLE, WAR IS HIS VENGEANCE; SO THAT HERE MEN ARE PUNISH'D FOR BEFORE-BREACH OF THE KING'S LAWS IN NOW THE KING'S QUARREL. WHERE THEY FEARED THE DEATH, THEY HAVE BORNE LIFE AWAY; AND WHERE THEY WOULD BE SAFE, THEY PERISH.
THEN IF THEY DIE UNPROVIDED, NO MORE IS THE KING GUILTY OF THEIR DAMNATION THAN HE WAS BEFORE GUILTY OF THOSE IMPIETIES FOR THE WHICH THEY ARE NOW VISITED.
EVERY SUBJECT'S DUTY IS THE KING'S; BUT EVERY SUBJECT'S SOUL IS HIS OWN. THEREFORE SHOULD EVERY SOLDIER IN THE WARS DO AS EVERY SICK MAN IN HIS BED, WASH EVERY MOTE OUT OF HIS CONSCIENCE; AND DYING SO, DEATH IS TO HIM ADVANTAGE; OR NOT DYING, THE TIME WAS BLESSEDLY LOST WHEREIN SUCH PREPARATION WAS GAINED;
AND IN HIM THAT ESCAPES, IT WERE NOT SIN TO THINK THAT, MAKING GOD SO FREE AN OFFER, HE LET HIM OUTLIVE THAT DAY TO SEE HIS GREATNESS, AND TO TEACH OTHERS HOW THEY SHOULD PREPARE.
'TIS CERTAIN, EVERY MAN THAT DIES ILL, THE ILL UPON HIS OWN HEAD: THE KING IS NOT TO ANSWER IT.

I DO NOT DESIRE HE SHOULD ANSWER FOR ME; AND YET I DETERMINE TO FIGHT LUSTILY FOR HIM.
I MYSELF HEARD THE KING SAY HE WOULD NOT BE RANSOM'D.
AY, HE SAID SO, TO MAKE US FIGHT CHEERFULLY; BUT WHEN OUR THROATS ARE CUT, HE MAY BE RANSOM'D, AND WE NE'ER THE WISER.
IF I LIVE TO SEE IT, I WILL NEVER TRUST HIS WORD AFTER.
YOU PAY HIM THEN! THAT'S A PERILOUS SHOT OUT OF AN ELDER-GUN, THAT A POOR AND A PRIVATE DISPLEASURE CAN DO AGAINST A MONARCH.
YOU MAY AS WELL GO ABOUT TO TURN THE SUN TO ICE WITH FANNING IN HIS FACE WITH A PEACOCK'S FEATHER. YOU'LL NEVER TRUST HIS WORD AFTER! COME, 'TIS A FOOLISH SAYING.
YOUR REPROOF IS SOMETHING TOO ROUND. I SHOULD BE ANGRY WITH YOU, IF THE TIME WERE CONVENIENT.
LET IT BE A QUARREL BETWEEN US IF YOU LIVE.
I EMBRACE IT.
HOW SHALL I KNOW THEE AGAIN?
GIVE ME ANY GAGE OF THINE, AND I WILL WEAR IT IN MY BONNET; THEN, IF EVER THOU DAR'ST ACKNOWLEDGE IT, I WILL MAKE IT MY QUARREL.
HERE'S MY GLOVE; GIVE ME ANOTHER OF THINE.
THERE.
THIS WILL I ALSO WEAR IN MY CAP. IF EVER THOU COME TO ME AND SAY, AFTER TO-MORROW, "THIS IS MY GLOVE," BY THIS HAND, I WILL TAKE THEE A BOX ON THE EAR.
IF EVER I LIVE TO SEE IT, I WILL CHALLENGE IT.

THOU DAR'ST AS WELL BE HANG'D.
WELL, I WILL DO IT, THOUGH I TAKE THEE IN THE KING'S COMPANY.
KEEP THY WORD; FARE THEE WELL.
BE FRIENDS, YOU ENGLISH FOOLS, BE FRIENDS. WE HAVE FRENCH QUARRELS ENOW, IF YOU COULD TELL HOW TO RECKON.
INDEED, THE FRENCH MAY LAY TWENTY FRENCH CROWNS TO ONE THEY WILL BEAT US, FOR THEY BEAR THEM ON THEIR SHOULDERS;
BUT IT IS NO ENGLISH TREASON TO CUT FRENCH CROWNS, AND TO-MORROW THE KING HIMSELF WILL BE A CLIPPER.

UPON THE KING! LET US OUR LIVES, OUR SOULS, OUR DEBTS, OUR CAREFUL WIVES, OUR CHILDREN, AND OUR SINS LAY ON THE KING!
WE MUST BEAR ALL. O HARD CONDITION, TWIN-BORN WITH GREATNESS, SUBJECT TO THE BREATH OF EVERY FOOL, WHOSE SENSE NO MORE CAN FEEL BUT HIS OWN WRINGING! WHAT INFINITE HEART'S EASE MUST KINGS NEGLECT, THAT PRIVATE MEN ENJOY!

AND WHAT HAVE KINGS, THAT PRIVATES HAVE NOT TOO, SAVE CEREMONY, SAVE GENERAL CEREMONY? AND WHAT ART THOU, THOU IDOL CEREMONY? WHAT KIND OF GOD ART THOU, THAT SUFFER'ST MORE OF MORTAL GRIEFS THAN DO THY WORSHIPPERS? WHAT ARE THY RENTS? WHAT ARE THY COMINGS-IN?
O CEREMONY, SHOW ME BUT THY WORTH! WHAT IS THY SOUL OF ADORATION? ART THOU AUGHT ELSE BUT PLACE, DEGREE, AND FORM, CREATING AWE AND FEAR IN OTHER MEN?
WHEREIN THOU ART LESS HAPPY, BEING FEAR'D, THAN THEY IN FEARING. WHAT DRINK'ST THOU OFT, INSTEAD OF HOMAGE SWEET, BUT POISON'D FLATTERY? O! BE SICK, GREAT GREATNESS, AND BID THY CEREMONY GIVE THEE CURE.
THINK'ST THOU THE FIERY FEVER WILL GO OUT WITH TITLES BLOWN FROM ADULATION? WILL IT GIVE PLACE TO FLEXURE AND LOW BENDING? CANST THOU, WHEN THOU COMMAND'ST THE BEGGAR'S KNEE, COMMAND THE HEALTH OF IT?

NO, THOU PROUD DREAM, THAT PLAY'ST SO SUBTLY WITH A KING'S REPOSE;
I AM A KING THAT FIND THEE, AND I KNOW 'TIS NOT THE BALM, THE SCEPTRE, AND THE BALL, THE SWORD, THE MACE, THE CROWN IMPERIAL, THE INTER-TISSUED ROBE OF GOLD AND PEARL, THE FARCED TITLE RUNNING 'FORE THE KING, THE THRONE HE SITS ON, NOR THE TIDE OF POMP THAT BEATS UPON THE HIGH SHORE OF THIS WORLD;

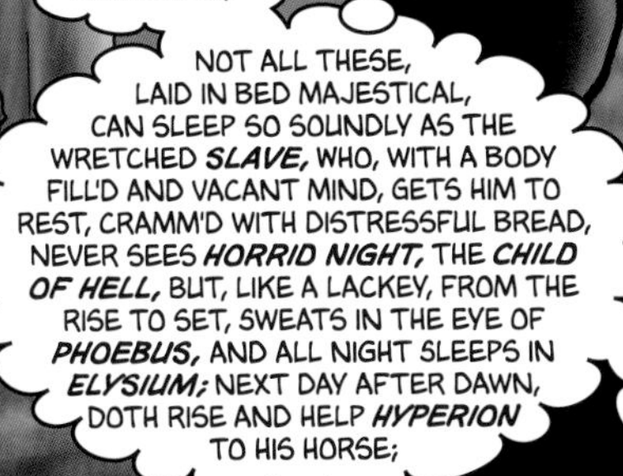
NO, NOT ALL THESE, THRICE-GORGEOUS CEREMONY,
NOT ALL THESE, LAID IN BED MAJESTICAL, CAN SLEEP SO SOUNDLY AS THE WRETCHED SLAVE, WHO, WITH A BODY FILL'D AND VACANT MIND, GETS HIM TO REST, CRAMM'D WITH DISTRESSFUL BREAD, NEVER SEES HORRID NIGHT, THE CHILD OF HELL, BUT, LIKE A LACKEY, FROM THE RISE TO SET, SWEATS IN THE EYE OF PHOEBUS, AND ALL NIGHT SLEEPS IN ELYSIUM; NEXT DAY AFTER DAWN, DOTH RISE AND HELP HYPERION TO HIS HORSE;

AND FOLLOWS SO THE EVER-RUNNING YEAR, WITH PROFITABLE LABOUR, TO HIS GRAVE:

AND, BUT FOR CEREMONY, SUCH A WRETCH, WINDING UP DAYS WITH TOIL AND NIGHTS WITH SLEEP, HAD THE FOREHAND AND VANTAGE OF A KING. THE SLAVE, A MEMBER OF THE COUNTRY'S PEACE, ENJOYS IT; BUT IN GROSS BRAIN LITTLE WOTS WHAT WATCH THE KING KEEPS TO MAINTAIN THE PEACE, WHOSE HOURS THE PEASANT BEST ADVANTAGES.
MY LORD, YOUR NOBLES, JEALOUS OF YOUR ABSENCE, SEEK THROUGH YOUR CAMP TO FIND YOU.
GOOD OLD KNIGHT, COLLECT THEM ALL TOGETHER AT MY TENT. I'LL BE BEFORE THEE.
I SHALL DO'T, MY LORD.

O GOD OF BATTLES! STEEL MY SOLDIERS' HEARTS. POSSESS THEM NOT WITH FEAR. TAKE FROM THEM NOW THE SENSE OF RECKONING, IF THE OPPOSED NUMBERS PLUCK THEIR HEARTS FROM THEM!
NOT TO-DAY, O LORD! O! NOT TO-DAY, THINK NOT UPON THE FAULT MY FATHER MADE IN COMPASSING THE CROWN. I RICHARD'S BODY HAVE INTERRED NEW, AND ON IT HAVE BESTOW'D MORE CONTRITE TEARS THAN FROM IT ISSUED FORCED DROPS OF BLOOD.
FIVE HUNDRED POOR I HAVE IN YEARLY PAY, WHO TWICE A DAY THEIR WITHER'D HANDS HOLD UP TOWARD HEAVEN, TO PARDON BLOOD;
AND I HAVE BUILT TWO CHANTRIES, WHERE THE SAD AND SOLEMN PRIESTS SING STILL FOR RICHARD'S SOUL. MORE WILL I DO; THOUGH ALL THAT I CAN DO IS NOTHING WORTH, SINCE THAT MY PENITENCE COMES AFTER ALL, IMPLORING PARDON.
MY LIEGE!
MY BROTHER GLOUCESTER'S VOICE?
AY; I KNOW THY ERRAND, I WILL GO WITH THEE:
THE DAY, MY FRIENDS, AND ALL THINGS STAY FOR ME.

Act Four
Scene Two
THE FRENCH CAMP AT AGINCOURT - 25TH OCTOBER 1415. THE MORNING OF THE BATTLE...
THE SUN DOTH GILD OUR ARMOUR; UP, MY LORDS!
MONTEZ À CHEVAL!
MY HORSE, VARLET! LAQUAIS! HA!
O BRAVE SPIRIT!
VIA! -- LES EAUX ET LA TERRE.
RIEN PUIS? L'AIR ET LE FEU.
CIEL, COUSIN ORLEANS. NOW, MY LORD CONSTABLE!
HARK, HOW OUR STEEDS FOR PRESENT SERVICE NEIGH!
MOUNT THEM, AND MAKE INCISION IN THEIR HIDES, THAT THEIR HOT BLOOD MAY SPIN IN ENGLISH EYES, AND DOUT THEM WITH SUPERFLUOUS COURAGE, HA!
WHAT, WILL YOU HAVE THEM WEEP OUR HORSES' BLOOD? HOW SHALL WE THEN BEHOLD THEIR NATURAL TEARS?

THE ENGLISH ARE EMBATTLED, YOU FRENCH PEERS.
TO HORSE, YOU GALLANT PRINCES! STRAIGHT TO HORSE! DO BUT BEHOLD YON POOR AND STARVED BAND, AND YOUR FAIR SHOW SHALL SUCK AWAY THEIR SOULS, LEAVING THEM BUT THE SHALES AND HUSKS OF MEN.
THERE IS NOT WORK ENOUGH FOR ALL OUR HANDS; SCARCE BLOOD ENOUGH IN ALL THEIR SICKLY VEINS TO GIVE EACH NAKED CURTLE-AXE A STAIN, THAT OUR FRENCH GALLANTS SHALL TO-DAY DRAW OUT, AND SHEATHE FOR LACK OF SPORT. LET US BUT BLOW ON THEM, THE VAPOUR OF OUR VALOUR WILL O'ERTURN THEM.
'TIS POSITIVE 'GAINST ALL EXCEPTIONS, LORDS, THAT OUR SUPERFLUOUS LACKEYS AND OUR PEASANTS, WHO, IN UNNECESSARY ACTION, SWARM ABOUT OUR SQUARES OF BATTLE, WERE ENOW TO PURGE THIS FIELD OF SUCH A HILDING FOE, THOUGH WE UPON THIS MOUNTAIN'S BASIS BY TOOK STAND FOR IDLE SPECULATION, BUT THAT OUR HONOURS MUST NOT. WHAT'S TO SAY? A VERY LITTLE LITTLE LET US DO, AND ALL IS DONE.
TAN-TARA!
TAN-TARA!
THEN LET THE TRUMPETS SOUND THE TUCKET SONANCE AND THE NOTE TO MOUNT; FOR OUR APPROACH SHALL SO MUCH DARE THE FIELD, THAT ENGLAND SHALL CROUCH DOWN IN FEAR, AND YIELD.
WHY DO YOU STAY SO LONG, MY LORDS OF FRANCE? YON ISLAND CARRIONS, DESPERATE OF THEIR BONES, ILL-FAVOUR'DLY BECOME THE MORNING FIELD.

THEIR RAGGED CURTAINS POORLY ARE LET LOOSE, AND OUR AIR SHAKES THEM PASSING SCORNFULLY.
BIG MARS SEEMS BANKRUPT IN THEIR BEGGAR'D HOST, AND FAINTLY THROUGH A RUSTY BEAVER PEEPS; THE HORSEMEN SIT LIKE FIXED CANDLESTICKS WITH TORCH-STAVES IN THEIR HAND; AND THEIR POOR JADES LOB DOWN THEIR HEADS, DROOPING THE HIDES AND HIPS, THE GUM DOWN-ROPING FROM THEIR PALE-DEAD EYES,
AND IN THEIR PALE DULL MOUTHS THE GIMMAL'D BIT LIES FOUL WITH CHEW'D GRASS, STILL, AND MOTIONLESS; AND THEIR EXECUTORS, THE KNAVISH CROWS, FLY O'ER THEM, ALL IMPATIENT FOR THEIR HOUR. DESCRIPTION CANNOT SUIT ITSELF IN WORDS TO DEMONSTRATE THE LIFE OF SUCH A BATTLE, IN LIFE SO LIFELESS AS IT SHOWS ITSELF.
THEY HAVE SAID THEIR PRAYERS, AND THEY STAY FOR DEATH.
SHALL WE GO SEND THEM DINNERS, AND FRESH SUITS, AND GIVE THEIR FASTING HORSES PROVENDER, AND AFTER FIGHT WITH THEM?
I STAY BUT FOR MY GUARD. ON, TO THE FIELD! I WILL THE BANNER FROM A TRUMPET TAKE, AND USE IT FOR MY HASTE. COME, COME, AWAY! THE SUN IS HIGH, AND WE OUTWEAR THE DAY.

Act Four
Scene Three
THE ENGLISH CAMP, AGINCOURT - 25TH OCTOBER 1415. THE MORNING OF THE BATTLE...
WHERE IS THE KING?
THE KING HIMSELF IS RODE TO VIEW THEIR BATTLE.
OF FIGHTING MEN THEY HAVE FULL THREE-SCORE THOUSAND.
THERE'S FIVE TO ONE; BESIDES, THEY ALL ARE FRESH.
GOD'S ARM STRIKE WITH US! 'TIS A FEARFUL ODDS.
GOD BE WI' YOU, PRINCES ALL; I'LL TO MY CHARGE. IF WE NO MORE MEET, TILL WE MEET IN HEAVEN, THEN, JOYFULLY,
MY NOBLE LORD OF BEDFORD, -- MY DEAR LORD GLOUCESTER, -- AND MY GOOD LORD EXETER, -- AND MY KIND KINSMAN, -- WARRIORS ALL, ADIEU!
FAREWELL, GOOD SALISBURY, AND GOOD LUCK GO WITH THEE!
FAREWELL, KIND LORD. FIGHT VALIANTLY TO-DAY! AND YET I DO THEE WRONG TO MIND THEE OF IT, FOR THOU ART FRAM'D OF THE FIRM TRUTH OF VALOUR.

HE IS AS FULL OF VALOUR AS OF KINDNESS; PRINCELY IN BOTH.
O! THAT WE NOW HAD HERE BUT ONE TEN THOUSAND OF THOSE MEN IN ENGLAND, THAT DO NO WORK TO-DAY!
WHAT'S HE THAT WISHES SO? MY COUSIN WESTMORELAND? -- NO, MY FAIR COUSIN. IF WE ARE MARK'D TO DIE, WE ARE ENOW TO DO OUR COUNTRY LOSS; AND IF TO LIVE, THE FEWER MEN, THE GREATER SHARE OF HONOUR.
GOD'S WILL! I PRAY THEE, WISH NOT ONE MAN MORE.

BY JOVE, I AM NOT COVETOUS FOR GOLD, NOR CARE I WHO DOTH FEED UPON MY COST;
IT YEARNS ME NOT IF MEN MY GARMENTS WEAR; SUCH OUTWARD THINGS DWELL NOT IN MY DESIRES;
BUT, IF IT BE A SIN TO COVET HONOUR, I AM THE MOST OFFENDING SOUL ALIVE. NO, FAITH, MY COZ, WISH NOT A MAN FROM ENGLAND.
GOD'S PEACE! I WOULD NOT LOSE SO GREAT AN HONOUR, AS ONE MAN MORE, METHINKS, WOULD SHARE FROM ME FOR THE BEST HOPE I HAVE. O! DO NOT WISH ONE MORE!
RATHER PROCLAIM IT, WESTMORELAND, THROUGH MY HOST, THAT HE WHICH HATH NO STOMACH TO THIS FIGHT, LET HIM DEPART; HIS PASSPORT SHALL BE MADE, AND CROWNS FOR CONVOY PUT INTO HIS PURSE.
WE WOULD NOT DIE IN THAT MAN'S COMPANY THAT FEARS HIS FELLOWSHIP TO DIE WITH US.
THIS DAY IS CALL'D THE FEAST OF CRISPIAN.
HE THAT OUTLIVES THIS DAY, AND COMES SAFE HOME, WILL STAND A TIP-TOE WHEN THIS DAY IS NAMED, AND ROUSE HIM AT THE NAME OF CRISPIAN. HE THAT SHALL LIVE THIS DAY, AND SEE OLD AGE, WILL YEARLY ON THE VIGIL FEAST HIS NEIGHBOURS, AND SAY, "TO-MORROW IS SAINT CRISPIAN."
THEN WILL HE STRIP HIS SLEEVE AND SHOW HIS SCARS, AND SAY, "THESE WOUNDS I HAD ON CRISPIAN'S DAY." OLD MEN FORGET; YET ALL SHALL BE FORGOT, BUT HE'LL REMEMBER WITH ADVANTAGES WHAT FEATS HE DID THAT DAY.

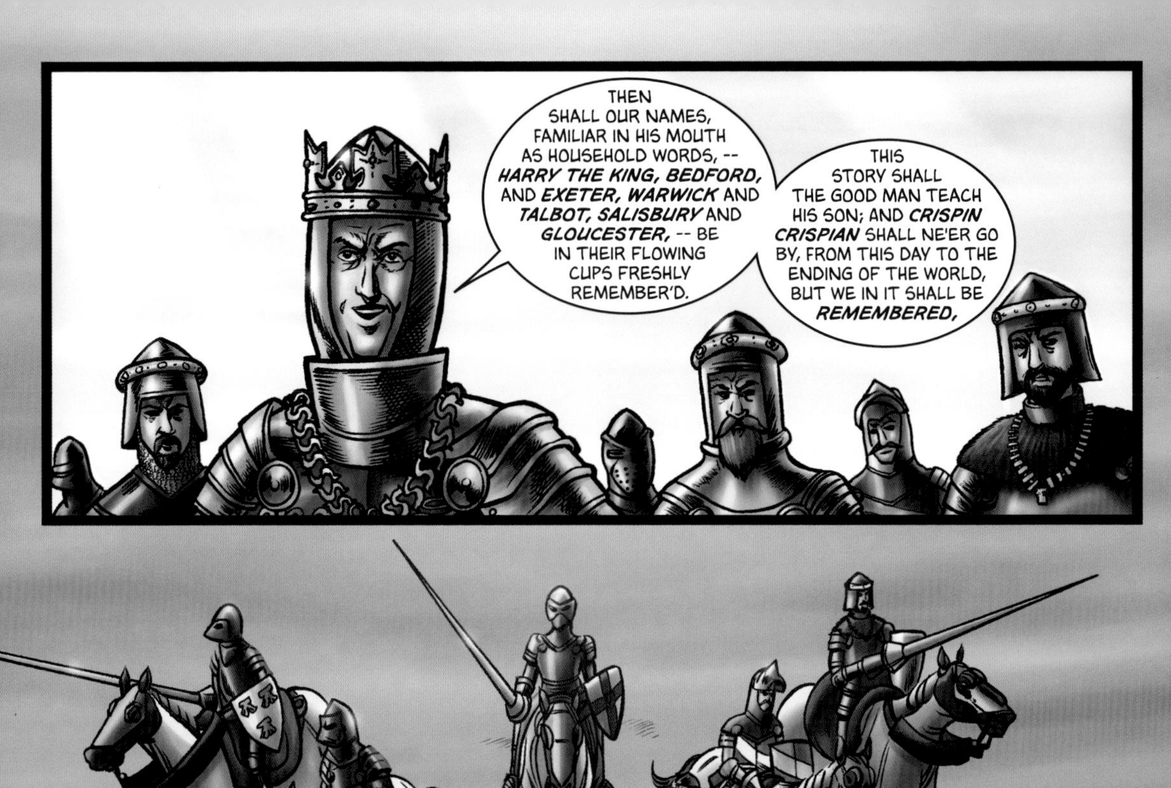
THEN SHALL OUR NAMES, FAMILIAR IN HIS MOUTH AS HOUSEHOLD WORDS, -- *HARRY THE KING, BEDFORD,* AND *EXETER, WARWICK* AND *TALBOT, SALISBURY* AND *GLOUCESTER,* -- BE IN THEIR FLOWING CUPS FRESHLY REMEMBER'D.
THIS STORY SHALL THE GOOD MAN TEACH HIS SON; AND *CRISPIN CRISPIAN* SHALL NE'ER GO BY, FROM THIS DAY TO THE ENDING OF THE WORLD, BUT WE IN IT SHALL BE *REMEMBERED,*

WE FEW, WE HAPPY FEW, WE *BAND OF BROTHERS.*
FOR HE TO-DAY THAT SHEDS HIS *BLOOD* WITH ME SHALL *BE* MY BROTHER; BE HE NE'ER SO VILE, THIS DAY SHALL GENTLE HIS CONDITION;
AND GENTLEMEN IN ENGLAND, NOW A-BED, SHALL THINK THEMSELVES *ACCURS'D* THEY WERE NOT HERE, AND HOLD THEIR MANHOODS *CHEAP,* WHILES ANY SPEAKS THAT FOUGHT WITH US UPON *SAINT CRISPIN'S DAY.*

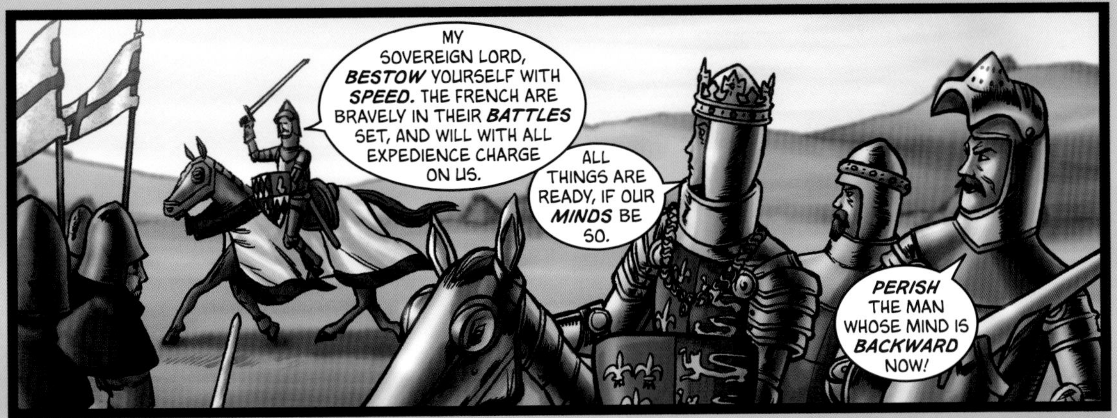
MY SOVEREIGN LORD, BESTOW YOURSELF WITH SPEED. THE FRENCH ARE BRAVELY IN THEIR BATTLES SET, AND WILL WITH ALL EXPEDIENCE CHARGE ON US.
ALL THINGS ARE READY, IF OUR MINDS BE SO.
PERISH THE MAN WHOSE MIND IS BACKWARD NOW!

THOU DOST NOT WISH MORE HELP FROM ENGLAND, COZ?
GOD'S WILL! MY LIEGE, WOULD YOU AND I ALONE, WITHOUT MORE HELP, COULD FIGHT THIS ROYAL BATTLE!
WHY, NOW THOU HAST UNWISH'D FIVE THOUSAND MEN, WHICH LIKES ME BETTER THAN TO WISH US ONE.

YOU KNOW YOUR PLACES. GOD BE WITH YOU ALL!
TAN-TARA!

ONCE MORE I COME TO KNOW OF THEE, KING HARRY, IF FOR THY RANSOM THOU WILT NOW COMPOUND, BEFORE THY MOST ASSURED OVERTHROW;
FOR, CERTAINLY, THOU ART SO NEAR THE GULF, THOU NEEDS MUST BE ENGLUTTED. BESIDES, IN MERCY, THE CONSTABLE DESIRES THEE, THOU WILT MIND THY FOLLOWERS OF REPENTANCE; THAT THEIR SOULS MAY MAKE A PEACEFUL AND A SWEET RETIRE FROM OFF THESE FIELDS, WHERE, WRETCHES, THEIR POOR BODIES MUST LIE AND FESTER.

WHO HATH SENT THEE NOW?
THE CONSTABLE OF FRANCE.
I PRAY THEE, BEAR MY FORMER ANSWER BACK:
BID THEM ACHIEVE ME AND THEN SELL MY BONES. GOOD GOD! WHY SHOULD THEY MOCK POOR FELLOWS THUS? THE MAN THAT ONCE DID SELL THE LION'S SKIN WHILE THE BEAST LIV'D, WAS KILL'D WITH HUNTING HIM.
A MANY OF OUR BODIES SHALL, NO DOUBT, FIND NATIVE GRAVES; UPON THE WHICH, I TRUST, SHALL WITNESS LIVE IN BRASS OF THIS DAY'S WORK;
AND THOSE THAT LEAVE THEIR VALIANT BONES IN FRANCE, DYING LIKE MEN, THOUGH BURIED IN YOUR DUNGHILLS, THEY SHALL BE FAM'D; FOR THERE THE SUN SHALL GREET THEM, AND DRAW THEIR HONOURS REEKING UP TO HEAVEN; LEAVING THEIR EARTHLY PARTS TO CHOKE YOUR CLIME, THE SMELL WHEREOF SHALL BREED A PLAGUE IN FRANCE.
MARK THEN ABOUNDING VALOUR IN OUR ENGLISH, THAT BEING DEAD, LIKE TO THE BULLET'S GRAZING, BREAK OUT INTO A SECOND COURSE OF MISCHIEF, KILLING IN RELAPSE OF MORTALITY.
LET ME SPEAK PROUDLY: -- TELL THE CONSTABLE WE ARE BUT WARRIORS FOR THE WORKING-DAY. OUR GAYNESS AND OUR GILT ARE ALL BESMIRCH'D WITH RAINY MARCHING IN THE PAINFUL FIELD; THERE'S NOT A PIECE OF FEATHER IN OUR HOST.

GOOD ARGUMENT, I HOPE, WE WILL NOT FLY -- AND TIME HATH WORN US INTO SLOVENRY; BUT, BY THE MASS, OUR HEARTS ARE IN THE TRIM;
AND MY POOR SOLDIERS TELL ME, YET ERE NIGHT THEY'LL BE IN FRESHER ROBES, OR THEY WILL PLUCK THE GAY NEW COATS O'ER THE FRENCH SOLDIERS' HEADS AND TURN THEM OUT OF SERVICE. IF THEY DO THIS -- AS, IF GOD PLEASE, THEY SHALL, -- MY RANSOM THEN WILL SOON BE LEVIED.
HERALD, SAVE THOU THY LABOUR. COME THOU NO MORE FOR RANSOM, GENTLE HERALD.
THEY SHALL HAVE NONE, I SWEAR, BUT THESE MY JOINTS; WHICH IF THEY HAVE AS I WILL LEAVE 'EM THEM, SHALL YIELD THEM LITTLE, TELL THE CONSTABLE.
I SHALL, KING HARRY. AND SO FARE THEE WELL; THOU NEVER SHALT HEAR HERALD ANY MORE.
I FEAR, THOU'LT ONCE MORE COME AGAIN FOR RANSOM.
MY LORD, MOST HUMBLY ON MY KNEE I BEG THE LEADING OF THE VAWARD.
TAKE IT, BRAVE YORK.
NOW, SOLDIERS, MARCH AWAY;
AND HOW THOU PLEASEST, GOD, DISPOSE THE DAY!

Act Four
Scene Four
THE BATTLE OF AGINCOURT.
25TH OCTOBER 1415...

YIELD, CUR!
JE PENSE QUE VOUS ÊTES LE GENTILHOMME DE BONNE QUALITÉ.
QUALITÉ? "CALENO CUSTORE ME!" ART THOU A GENTLEMAN? WHAT IS THY NAME? DISCUSS.
O SEIGNEUR DIEU!
O, Signieur Dew should be a gentleman.
PERPEND MY WORDS, O SIGNIEUR DEW, AND MARK: O SIGNIEUR DEW, THOU DIEST ON POINT OF FOX, EXCEPT, O SIGNIEUR, THOU DO GIVE TO ME EGREGIOUS RANSOM.
O, PRENEZ MISÉRICORDE! AYEZ PITIÉ DE MOI!
MOY SHALL NOT SERVE; I WILL HAVE FORTY MOYS, OR I WILL FETCH THY RIM OUT AT THY THROAT IN DROPS OF CRIMSON BLOOD.
EST-IL IMPOSSIBLE D'ÉCHAPPER LA FORCE DE TON BRAS?

BRASS, CUR! THOU DAMNED AND LUXURIOUS MOUNTAIN GOAT, OFFER'ST ME BRASS?
O PARDONNEZ-MOI!
SAY'ST THOU ME SO? IS THAT A TON OF MOYS?

COME HITHER, BOY; ASK ME THIS SLAVE IN FRENCH WHAT IS HIS NAME.

ÉCOUTEZ: COMMENT ÊTES-VOUS APPELÉ?
MONSIEUR LE FER.

HE SAYS HIS NAME IS MASTER FER.
MASTER FER! I'LL FER HIM, AND FIRK HIM, AND FERRET HIM. -- DISCUSS THE SAME IN FRENCH UNTO HIM.

I DO NOT KNOW THE FRENCH FOR FER, AND FERRET, AND FIRK.
BID HIM PREPARE; FOR I WILL CUT HIS THROAT.

QUE DIT-IL, MONSIEUR?
IL ME COMMANDE À VOUS DIRE QUE VOUS FAITES VOUS PRÊT; CAR CE SOLDAT ICI EST DISPOSÉ TOUT À CETTE HEURE DE COUPER VOTRE GORGE.
OWY, CUPPELE GORGE, PERMAFOY, PEASANT, UNLESS THOU GIVE ME CROWNS, BRAVE CROWNS; OR MANGLED SHALT THOU BE BY THIS MY SWORD.

O, JE VOUS SUPPLIE, POUR L'AMOUR DE DIEU, ME PARDONNER! JE SUIS GENTILHOMME DE BONNE MAISON; GARDEZ MA VIE, ET JE VOUS DONNERAI DEUX CENTS ÉCUS.
WHAT ARE HIS WORDS?
HE PRAYS YOU TO SAVE HIS LIFE. HE IS A GENTLEMAN OF A GOOD HOUSE; AND FOR HIS RANSOM HE WILL GIVE YOU TWO HUNDRED CROWNS.

TELL HIM MY FURY SHALL ABATE, AND I THE CROWNS WILL TAKE.
PETIT MONSIEUR, QUE DIT-IL?
ENCORE QU'IL EST CONTRE SON JUREMENT DE PARDONNER AUCUN PRISONNIER; NÉANMOINS, POUR LES ÉCUS QUE VOUS L'AVEZ PROMIS, IL EST CONTENT À VOUS DONNER LA LIBERTÉ, LE FRANCHISEMENT.

SUR MES GENOUX JE VOUS DONNE MILLE REMERCIEMENTS; ET JE M'ESTIME HEUREUX QUE JE SUIS TOMBÉ ENTRE LES MAINS D'UN CHEVALIER, JE PENSE, LE PLUS BRAVE, VAILLANT, ET TRES DISTINGUÉ SEIGNEUR D'ANGLETERRE.
EXPOUND UNTO ME, BOY.
HE GIVES YOU, UPON HIS KNEES, A THOUSAND THANKS; AND HE ESTEEMS HIMSELF HAPPY THAT HE HATH FALLEN INTO THE HANDS OF ONE, AS HE THINKS, THE MOST BRAVE, VALOROUS, AND THRICE-WORTHY SIGNIEUR OF ENGLAND.
AS I SUCK BLOOD, I WILL SOME MERCY SHOW. FOLLOW ME!
SUIVEZ-VOUS LE GRAND CAPITAINE.
I DID NEVER KNOW SO FULL A VOICE ISSUE FROM SO EMPTY A HEART; BUT THE SAYING IS TRUE, "THE EMPTY VESSEL MAKES THE GREATEST SOUND."
BARDOLPH AND NYM HAD TEN TIMES MORE VALOUR THAN THIS ROARING DEVIL I' THE OLD PLAY, THAT EVERY ONE MAY PARE HIS NAILS WITH A WOODEN DAGGER;
AND THEY ARE BOTH HANG'D; AND SO WOULD THIS BE, IF HE DURST STEAL ANYTHING ADVENTUROUSLY.
I MUST STAY WITH THE LACKEYS, WITH THE LUGGAGE OF OUR CAMP. THE FRENCH MIGHT HAVE A GOOD PREY OF US, IF HE KNEW OF IT; FOR THERE IS NONE TO GUARD IT BUT BOYS.

Act Four
Scene Five
ON THE FRENCH SIDE OF THE BATTLEFIELD. THE FRENCH ARE LOSING...
O DIABLE!
O SEIGNEUR! LE JOUR EST PERDU, TOUT EST PERDU!
MORT DE MA VIE! ALL IS CONFOUNDED, ALL! REPROACH AND EVERLASTING SHAME SITS MOCKING IN OUR PLUMES. O MÉCHANTE FORTUNE!
TAN-TARA!
DO NOT RUN AWAY.
WHY, ALL OUR RANKS ARE BROKE.
O PERDURABLE SHAME! -- LET'S STAB OURSELVES, BE THESE THE WRETCHES THAT WE PLAY'D AT DICE FOR?
IS THIS THE KING WE SENT TO FOR HIS RANSOM?
SHAME AND ETERNAL SHAME, NOTHING BUT SHAME! LET'S DIE IN HONOUR! -- ONCE MORE BACK AGAIN! AND HE THAT WILL NOT FOLLOW BOURBON NOW, LET HIM GO HENCE, AND WITH HIS CAP IN HAND, LIKE A BASE PANDAR, HOLD THE CHAMBER DOOR WHILST BY A SLAVE, NO GENTLER THAN MY DOG, HIS FAIREST DAUGHTER IS CONTAMINATED.
DISORDER, THAT HATH SPOIL'D US, FRIEND US NOW! LET US, ON HEAPS, GO OFFER UP OUR LIVES.
WE ARE ENOUGH, YET LIVING IN THE FIELD, TO SMOTHER UP THE ENGLISH IN OUR THRONGS, IF ANY ORDER MIGHT BE THOUGHT UPON.
THE DEVIL TAKE ORDER NOW! I'LL TO THE THRONG. LET LIFE BE SHORT, ELSE SHAME WILL BE TOO LONG.

Act Four
Scene Six
THE BATTLE OF AGINCOURT CONTINUES...
WELL HAVE WE DONE, THRICE-VALIANT COUNTRYMEN. BUT ALL'S NOT DONE; YET KEEP THE FRENCH THE FIELD.
THE DUKE OF YORK COMMENDS HIM TO YOUR MAJESTY.
LIVES HE, GOOD UNCLE? THRICE WITHIN THIS HOUR I SAW HIM DOWN; THRICE UP AGAIN, AND FIGHTING. FROM HELMET TO THE SPUR ALL BLOOD HE WAS.
IN WHICH ARRAY, BRAVE SOLDIER, DOTH HE LIE, LARDING THE PLAIN;
AND BY HIS BLOODY SIDE, -- YOKE-FELLOW TO HIS HONOUR-OWING WOUNDS, -- THE NOBLE EARL OF SUFFOLK ALSO LIES.
SUFFOLK FIRST DIED; AND YORK, ALL HAGGLED OVER, COMES TO HIM, WHERE IN GORE HE LAY INSTEEP'D, AND TAKES HIM BY THE BEARD; KISSES THE GASHES, THAT BLOODILY DID YAWN UPON HIS FACE.

HE CRIES ALOUD, "TARRY, MY COUSIN SUFFOLK! MY SOUL SHALL THINE KEEP COMPANY TO HEAVEN; TARRY, SWEET SOUL, FOR MINE, THEN FLY ABREAST, AS IN THIS GLORIOUS AND WELL-FOUGHTEN FIELD WE KEPT TOGETHER IN OUR CHIVALRY." UPON THESE WORDS I CAME AND CHEER'D HIM UP. HE SMIL'D ME IN THE FACE, RAUGHT ME HIS HAND, AND, WITH A FEEBLE GRIPE, SAYS, "DEAR MY LORD, COMMEND MY SERVICE TO MY SOVEREIGN."
SO DID HE TURN AND OVER SUFFOLK'S NECK HE THREW HIS WOUNDED ARM AND KISS'D HIS LIPS; AND SO ESPOUS'D TO DEATH, WITH BLOOD HE SEAL'D A TESTAMENT OF NOBLE-ENDING LOVE. THE PRETTY AND SWEET MANNER OF IT FORC'D THOSE WATERS FROM ME, WHICH I WOULD HAVE STOPP'D;
BUT I HAD NOT SO MUCH OF MAN IN ME, AND ALL MY MOTHER CAME INTO MINE EYES AND GAVE ME UP TO TEARS.
I BLAME YOU NOT; FOR, HEARING THIS, I MUST PERFORCE COMPOUND WITH MISTFUL EYES, OR THEY WILL ISSUE TOO.
TAN-TARA!
BUT HARK! WHAT NEW ALARUM IS THIS SAME?
THE FRENCH HAVE REINFORC'D THEIR SCATTER'D MEN. THEN, EVERY SOLDIER KILL HIS PRISONERS!
GIVE THE WORD THROUGH.

Act Four
Scene Seven
THE ENGLISH CAMP, AGINCOURT. THE CAMP IS DESTROYED...
KILL THE POYS AND THE LUGGAGE! 'TIS EXPRESSLY AGAINST THE LAW OF ARMS. 'TIS AS ARRANT A PIECE OF KNAVERY, MARK YOU NOW, AS CAN BE OFFER'T; IN YOUR CONSCIENCE, NOW, IS IT NOT?
'TIS CERTAIN THERE'S NOT A BOY LEFT ALIVE; AND THE COWARDLY RASCALS THAT RAN FROM THE BATTLE HA' DONE THIS SLAUGHTER.
BESIDES, THEY HAVE BURNED AND CARRIED AWAY ALL THAT WAS IN THE KING'S TENT; WHEREFORE THE KING, MOST WORTHILY, HATH CAUS'D EVERY SOLDIER TO CUT HIS PRISONER'S THROAT.
O, 'TIS A GALLANT KING!
AY, HE WAS PORN AT MONMOUTH, CAPTAIN GOWER. WHAT CALL YOU THE TOWN'S NAME WHERE ALEXANDER THE PIG WAS BORN?
ALEXANDER THE GREAT.
WHY, I PRAY YOU, IS NOT PIG GREAT? THE PIG, OR THE GREAT, OR THE MIGHTY, OR THE HUGE, OR THE MAGNANIMOUS, ARE ALL ONE RECKONINGS, SAVE THE PHRASE IS A LITTLE VARIATIONS.
I THINK ALEXANDER THE GREAT WAS BORN IN MACEDON. HIS FATHER WAS CALLED PHILIP OF MACEDON, AS I TAKE IT.

I THINK IT IS IN MACEDON WHERE ALEXANDER IS PORN. I TELL YOU, CAPTAIN, IF YOU LOOK IN THE MAPS OF THE 'ORLD, I WARRANT, YOU SHALL FIND, IN THE COMPARISONS BETWEEN MACEDON AND MONMOUTH, THAT THE SITUATIONS, LOOK YOU, IS BOTH ALIKE.
THERE IS A RIVER IN MACEDON; AND THERE IS ALSO MOREOVER A RIVER AT MONMOUTH; IT IS CALL'D WYE AT MONMOUTH;

BUT IT IS OUT OF MY PRAINS WHAT IS THE NAME OF THE OTHER RIVER; BUT 'TIS ALL ONE, 'TIS ALIKE AS MY FINGERS IS TO MY FINGERS, AND THERE IS SALMONS IN BOTH. IF YOU MARK ALEXANDER'S LIFE WELL, HARRY OF MONMOUTH'S LIFE IS COME AFTER IT INDIFFERENT WELL; FOR THERE IS FIGURES IN ALL THINGS.

ALEXANDER, GOD KNOWS, AND YOU KNOW, IN HIS RAGES, AND HIS FURIES, AND HIS WRATHS, AND HIS CHOLERS, AND HIS MOODS, AND HIS DISPLEASURES, AND HIS INDIGNATIONS, AND ALSO BEING A LITTLE INTOXICATE IN HIS PRAINS, DID, IN HIS ALES AND HIS ANGERS, LOOK YOU, KILL HIS BEST FRIEND, CLEITUS.
OUR KING IS NOT LIKE HIM IN THAT. HE NEVER KILL'D ANY OF HIS FRIENDS.

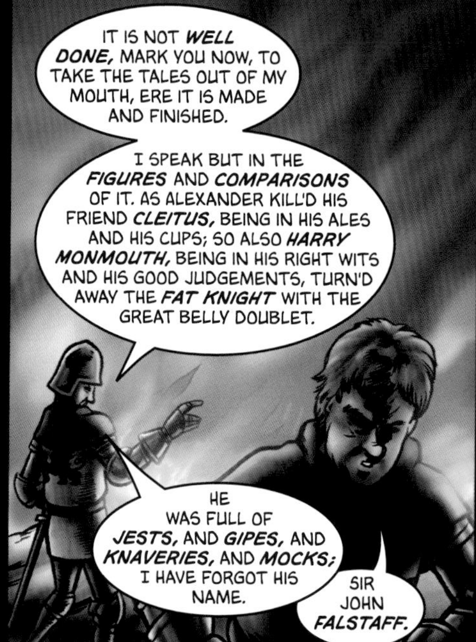
IT IS NOT WELL DONE, MARK YOU NOW, TO TAKE THE TALES OUT OF MY MOUTH, ERE IT IS MADE AND FINISHED.
I SPEAK BUT IN THE FIGURES AND COMPARISONS OF IT. AS ALEXANDER KILL'D HIS FRIEND CLEITUS, BEING IN HIS ALES AND HIS CUPS; SO ALSO HARRY MONMOUTH, BEING IN HIS RIGHT WITS AND HIS GOOD JUDGEMENTS, TURN'D AWAY THE FAT KNIGHT WITH THE GREAT BELLY DOUBLET.
HE WAS FULL OF JESTS, AND GIPES, AND KNAVERIES, AND MOCKS; I HAVE FORGOT HIS NAME.
SIR JOHN FALSTAFF.

THAT IS HE. I'LL TELL YOU THERE IS GOOD MEN PORN AT MONMOUTH.
HERE COMES HIS MAJESTY.

I WAS NOT ANGRY SINCE I CAME TO FRANCE UNTIL THIS INSTANT.
TAKE A TRUMPET, HERALD; RIDE THOU UNTO THE HORSEMEN ON YON HILL. IF THEY WILL FIGHT WITH US, BID THEM COME DOWN, OR VOID THE FIELD; THEY DO OFFEND OUR SIGHT. IF THEY'LL DO NEITHER, WE WILL COME TO THEM, AND MAKE THEM SKIRR AWAY, AS SWIFT AS STONES ENFORCED FROM THE OLD ASSYRIAN SLINGS.
BESIDES, WE'LL CUT THE THROATS OF THOSE WE HAVE, AND NOT A MAN OF THEM THAT WE SHALL TAKE SHALL TASTE OUR MERCY.
GO AND TELL THEM SO.
HERE COMES THE HERALD OF THE FRENCH, MY LIEGE.
HIS EYES ARE HUMBLER THAN THEY US'D TO BE.
HOW NOW! WHAT MEANS THIS, HERALD? KNOW'ST THOU NOT THAT I HAVE FIN'D THESE BONES OF MINE FOR RANSOM? COM'ST THOU AGAIN FOR RANSOM?
NO, GREAT KING;
I COME TO THEE FOR CHARITABLE LICENSE, THAT WE MAY WANDER O'ER THIS BLOODY FIELD TO BOOK OUR DEAD, AND THEN TO BURY THEM;

TO SORT OUR NOBLES FROM OUR COMMON MEN. FOR MANY OF OUR PRINCES -- WOE THE WHILE! -- LIE DROWN'D AND SOAK'D IN MERCENARY BLOOD;
SO DO OUR VULGAR DRENCH THEIR PEASANT LIMBS IN BLOOD OF PRINCES;
AND THEIR WOUNDED STEEDS FRET FETLOCK DEEP IN GORE, AND WITH WILD RAGE YERK OUT THEIR ARMED HEELS AT THEIR DEAD MASTERS, KILLING THEM TWICE.
O! GIVE US LEAVE, GREAT KING, TO VIEW THE FIELD IN SAFETY, AND DISPOSE OF THEIR DEAD BODIES.
I TELL THEE TRULY, HERALD, I KNOW NOT IF THE DAY BE OURS, OR NO; FOR YET A MANY OF YOUR HORSEMEN PEER AND GALLOP O'ER THE FIELD.
THE DAY IS YOURS.
PRAISED BE GOD, AND NOT OUR STRENGTH, FOR IT!
WHAT IS THIS CASTLE CALL'D THAT STANDS HARD BY?
THEY CALL IT AGINCOURT.
THEN CALL WE THIS THE FIELD OF AGINCOURT, FOUGHT ON THE DAY OF CRISPIN CRISPIANUS.
YOUR GRANDFATHER OF FAMOUS MEMORY, AN'T PLEASE YOUR MAJESTY, AND YOUR GREAT-UNCLE EDWARD THE PLACK PRINCE OF WALES, AS I HAVE READ IN THE CHRONICLES, FOUGHT A MOST PRAVE PATTLE HERE IN FRANCE.
THEY DID, FLUELLEN.
YOUR MAJESTY SAYS VERY TRUE. IF YOUR MAJESTIES IS REMEMBER'D OF IT, THE WELSHMEN DID GOOD SERVICE IN A GARDEN WHERE LEEKS DID GROW, WEARING LEEKS IN THEIR MONMOUTH CAPS;
WHICH, YOUR MAJESTY KNOW, TO THIS HOUR IS AN HONOURABLE BADGE OF THE SERVICE;
AND I DO BELIEVE YOUR MAJESTY TAKES NO SCORN TO WEAR THE LEEK UPON SAINT TAVY'S DAY.
I WEAR IT FOR A MEMORABLE HONOUR; FOR I AM WELSH, YOU KNOW, GOOD COUNTRYMAN.

ALL THE WATER IN WYE CANNOT WASH YOUR MAJESTY'S WELSH PLOOD OUT OF YOUR PODY, I CAN TELL YOU THAT. GOT PLESS IT, AND PRESERVE IT, AS LONG AS IT PLEASES HIS GRACE, AND HIS MAJESTY TOO!
THANKS, GOOD MY COUNTRY-MAN.

BY JESHU, I AM YOUR MAJESTY'S COUNTRYMAN, I CARE NOT WHO KNOW IT. I WILL CONFESS IT TO ALL THE 'ORLD.
I NEED NOT BE ASHAM'D OF YOUR MAJESTY, PRAISED BE GOD, SO LONG AS YOUR MAJESTY IS AN HONEST MAN.
GOD KEEP ME SO!

OUR HERALDS GO WITH HIM; BRING ME JUST NOTICE OF THE NUMBERS DEAD ON BOTH OUR PARTS.

CALL YONDER FELLOW HITHER.

SOLDIER, YOU MUST COME TO THE KING.

SOLDIER, WHY WEAR'ST THOU THAT GLOVE IN THY CAP?
AN'T PLEASE YOUR MAJESTY, 'TIS THE GAGE OF ONE THAT I SHOULD FIGHT WITHAL, IF HE BE ALIVE.
AN ENGLISH-MAN?
AN'T PLEASE YOUR MAJESTY, A RASCAL THAT SWAGGER'D WITH ME LAST NIGHT; WHO, IF 'A LIVE AND EVER DARE TO CHALLENGE THIS GLOVE, I HAVE SWORN TO TAKE HIM A BOX O' THE EAR; OR, IF I CAN SEE MY GLOVE IN HIS CAP, WHICH HE SWORE, AS HE WAS A SOLDIER, HE WOULD WEAR IF ALIVE, I WILL STRIKE IT OUT SOUNDLY.
WHAT THINK YOU, CAPTAIN FLUELLEN? IS IT FIT THIS SOLDIER KEEP HIS OATH?
HE IS A CRAVEN AND A VILLAIN ELSE, AN'T PLEASE YOUR MAJESTY, IN MY CONSCIENCE.

IT MAY BE HIS ENEMY IS A GENTLEMEN OF GREAT SORT, QUITE FROM THE ANSWER OF HIS DEGREE.
THOUGH HE BE AS GOOD A GENTLEMAN AS THE DEVIL IS, AS LUCIFER AND BELZEBUB HIMSELF, IT IS NECESSARY, LOOK YOUR GRACE, THAT HE KEEP HIS VOW AND HIS OATH. IF HE BE PERJUR'D, SEE YOU NOW, HIS REPUTATION IS AS ARRANT A VILLAIN AND A JACK-SAUCE, AS EVER HIS BLACK SHOE TROD UPON GOD'S GROUND AND HIS EARTH, IN MY CONSCIENCE, LA!

THEN KEEP THY VOW, SIRRAH, WHEN THOU MEET'ST THE FELLOW.
SO I WILL, MY LIEGE, AS I LIVE.
WHO SERV'ST THOU UNDER?
UNDER CAPTAIN GOWER, MY LIEGE.
GOWER IS A GOOD CAPTAIN, AND IS GOOD KNOWLEDGE AND LITERATURED IN THE WARS.
CALL HIM HITHER TO ME, SOLDIER.
I WILL, MY LIEGE.
HERE, FLUELLEN; WEAR THOU THIS FAVOUR FOR ME, AND STICK IT IN THY CAP. WHEN ALENÇON AND MYSELF WERE DOWN TOGETHER, I PLUCK'D THIS GLOVE FROM HIS HELM. IF ANY MAN CHALLENGE THIS, HE IS A FRIEND TO ALENÇON, AND AN ENEMY TO OUR PERSON. IF THOU ENCOUNTER ANY SUCH, APPREHEND HIM, AN THOU DOST ME LOVE.

YOUR GRACE DOES ME AS GREAT HONOURS AS CAN BE DESIR'D IN THE HEARTS OF HIS SUBJECTS.
I WOULD FAIN SEE THE MAN, THAT HAS BUT TWO LEGS, THAT SHALL FIND HIMSELF AGGRIEF'D AT THIS GLOVE; THAT IS ALL. BUT I WOULD FAIN SEE IT ONCE, AN PLEASE GOD OF HIS GRACE THAT I MIGHT SEE.
KNOW'ST THOU GOWER?
HE IS MY DEAR FRIEND, AN'T PLEASE YOU.
PRAY THEE, GO SEEK HIM, AND BRING HIM TO MY TENT.
I WILL FETCH HIM.

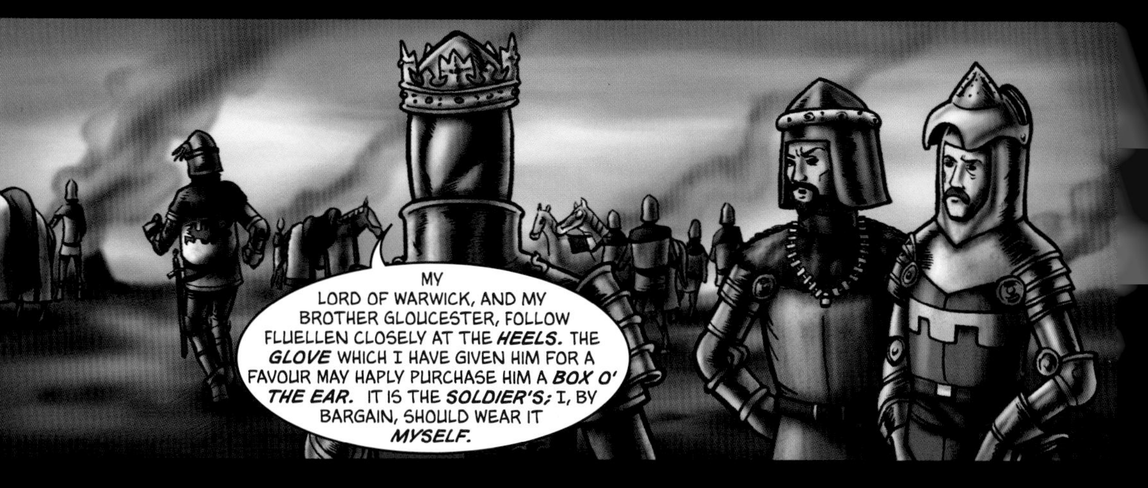
MY LORD OF WARWICK, AND MY BROTHER GLOUCESTER, FOLLOW FLUELLEN CLOSELY AT THE HEELS. THE GLOVE WHICH I HAVE GIVEN HIM FOR A FAVOUR MAY HAPLY PURCHASE HIM A BOX O' THE EAR. IT IS THE SOLDIER'S; I, BY BARGAIN, SHOULD WEAR IT MYSELF.

FOLLOW, GOOD COUSIN WARWICK. IF THAT THE SOLDIER STRIKE HIM -- AS, I JUDGE BY HIS BLUNT BEARING, HE WILL KEEP HIS WORD, -- SOME SUDDEN MISCHIEF MAY ARISE OF IT;
FOR I DO KNOW FLUELLEN VALIANT AND, TOUCH'D WITH CHOLER, HOT AS GUNPOWDER, AND QUICKLY WILL RETURN AN INJURY. FOLLOW, AND SEE THERE BE NO HARM BETWEEN THEM.

GO YOU WITH ME, UNCLE OF EXETER.

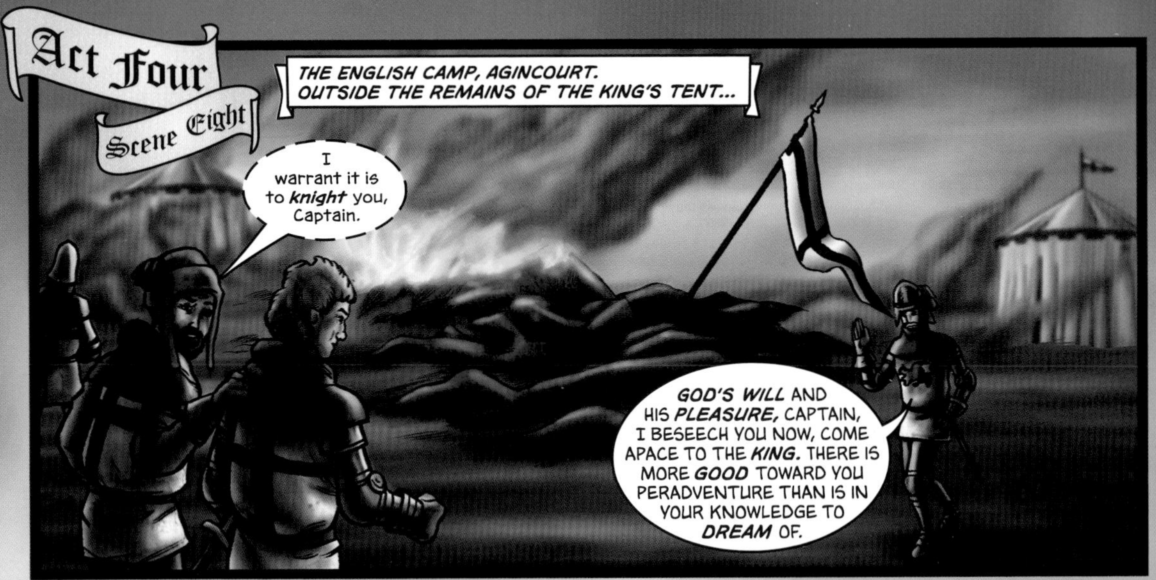
Act Four
Scene Eight
THE ENGLISH CAMP, AGINCOURT. OUTSIDE THE REMAINS OF THE KING'S TENT...
I warrant it is to knight you, Captain.
GOD'S WILL AND HIS PLEASURE, CAPTAIN, I BESEECH YOU NOW, COME APACE TO THE KING. THERE IS MORE GOOD TOWARD YOU PERADVENTURE THAN IS IN YOUR KNOWLEDGE TO DREAM OF.

SIR, KNOW YOU THIS GLOVE?
KNOW THE GLOVE? I KNOW THE GLOVE IS A GLOVE.

I KNOW THIS;

AND THUS I CHALLENGE IT.
SMAAAACK!!!
'SBLOOD! AN ARRANT TRAITOR AS ANY'S IN THE UNIVERSAL 'ORLD, OR IN FRANCE, OR IN ENGLAND!

HOW NOW, SIR! YOU VILLAIN!
DO YOU THINK I'LL BE FOR-SWORN?
STAND AWAY, CAPTAIN GOWER. I WILL GIVE TREASON HIS PAYMENT INTO PLOWS, I WARRANT YOU.

I AM NO TRAITOR.
THAT'S A LIE IN THY THROAT. -- I CHARGE YOU IN HIS MAJESTY'S NAME, APPREHEND HIM; HE'S A FRIEND OF THE DUKE ALENÇON'S.
HOW NOW, HOW NOW! WHAT'S THE MATTER?
MY LORD OF WARWICK, HERE IS -- PRAISED BE GOD FOR IT! -- A MOST CONTAGIOUS TREASON COME TO LIGHT, LOOK YOU, AS YOU SHALL DESIRE IN A SUMMER'S DAY. HERE IS HIS MAJESTY.
HOW NOW! WHAT'S THE MATTER?
MY LIEGE, HERE IS A VILLAIN AND A TRAITOR, THAT, LOOK YOUR GRACE, HAS STRUCK THE GLOVE WHICH YOUR MAJESTY IS TAKE OUT OF THE HELMET OF ALENÇON.
MY LIEGE, THIS WAS MY GLOVE;
HERE IS THE FELLOW OF IT; AND HE THAT I GAVE IT TO IN CHANGE PROMIS'D TO WEAR IT IN HIS CAP. I PROMIS'D TO STRIKE HIM, IF HE DID. I MET THIS MAN WITH MY GLOVE IN HIS CAP, AND I HAVE BEEN AS GOOD AS MY WORD.
YOUR MAJESTY HEAR NOW, SAVING YOUR MAJESTY'S MANHOOD, WHAT AN ARRANT, RASCALLY, BEGGARLY, LOUSY KNAVE IT IS. I HOPE YOUR MAJESTY IS PEAR ME TESTIMONY AND WITNESS, AND WILL AVOUCHMENT, THAT THIS IS THE GLOVE OF ALENÇON THAT YOUR MAJESTY IS GIVE ME; IN YOUR CONSCIENCE, NOW?
GIVE ME THY GLOVE, SOLDIER. LOOK, HERE IS THE FELLOW OF IT.
'TWAS I, INDEED, THOU PROMISEDST TO STRIKE; AND THOU HAST GIVEN ME MOST BITTER TERMS.
AN 'T PLEASE YOUR MAJESTY, LET HIS NECK ANSWER FOR IT, IF THERE IS ANY MARTIAL LAW IN THE 'ORLD.

HOW CANST THOU MAKE ME SATISFACTION?
ALL OFFENCES, MY LORD, COME FROM THE HEART. NEVER CAME ANY FROM MINE, THAT MIGHT OFFEND YOUR MAJESTY.
IT WAS OURSELF THOU DIDST ABUSE.
YOUR MAJESTY CAME NOT LIKE YOURSELF. YOU APPEAR'D TO ME BUT AS A COMMON MAN; WITNESS THE NIGHT, YOUR GARMENTS, YOUR LOWLINESS; AND WHAT YOUR HIGHNESS SUFFER'D UNDER THAT SHAPE, I BESEECH YOU TAKE IT FOR YOUR OWN FAULT AND NOT MINE;
FOR HAD YOU BEEN AS I TOOK YOU FOR, I MADE NO OFFENCE; THEREFORE, I BESEECH YOUR HIGHNESS, PARDON ME.

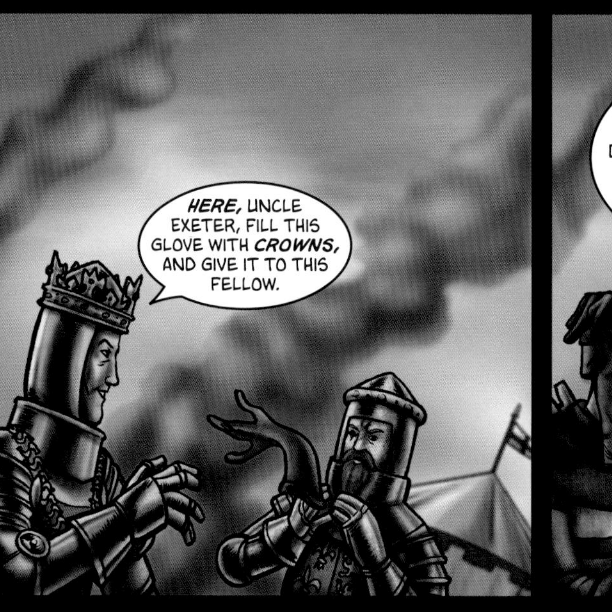
HERE, UNCLE EXETER, FILL THIS GLOVE WITH CROWNS, AND GIVE IT TO THIS FELLOW.

KEEP IT, FELLOW; AND WEAR IT FOR AN HONOUR IN THY CAP, TILL I DO CHALLENGE IT. -- GIVE HIM THE CROWNS; -- AND, CAPTAIN, YOU MUST NEEDS BE FRIENDS WITH HIM.
BY THIS DAY AND THIS LIGHT, THE FELLOW HAS METTLE ENOUGH IN HIS BELLY.

HOLD, THERE IS TWELVE PENCE FOR YOU; AND I PRAY YOU TO SERVE GOD, AND KEEP YOU OUT OF PRAWLS, AND PRABBLES, AND QUARRELS, AND DISSENSIONS; AND, I WARRANT YOU, IT IS THE BETTER FOR YOU.
I WILL NONE OF YOUR MONEY.

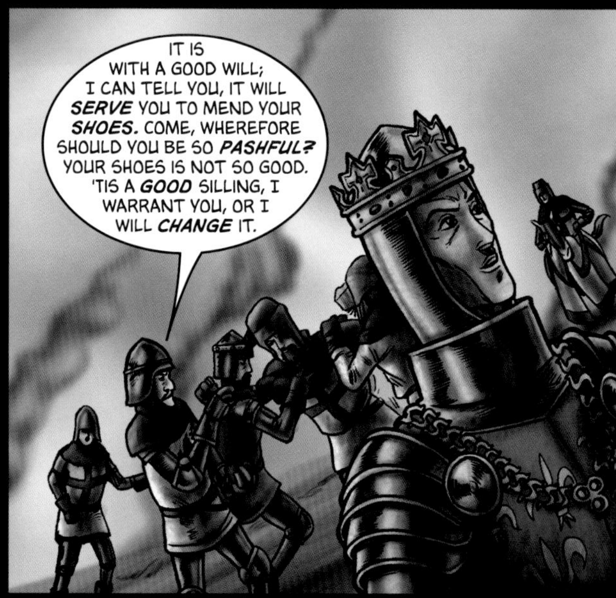
IT IS WITH A GOOD WILL; I CAN TELL YOU, IT WILL SERVE YOU TO MEND YOUR SHOES. COME, WHEREFORE SHOULD YOU BE SO PASHFUL? YOUR SHOES IS NOT SO GOOD. 'TIS A GOOD SILLING, I WARRANT YOU, OR I WILL CHANGE IT.

NOW, HERALD, ARE THE DEAD NUMB'RED?
HERE IS THE NUMBER OF THE SLAUGHT'RED FRENCH.

WHAT PRISONERS OF GOOD SORT ARE TAKEN, UNCLE?
CHARLES DUKE OF ORLEANS, NEPHEW TO THE KING; JOHN DUKE OF BOURBON, AND LORD BOUCIQUALT: OF OTHER LORDS AND BARONS, KNIGHTS AND SQUIRES, FULL FIFTEEN HUNDRED, BESIDES COMMON MEN.

THIS NOTE DOTH TELL ME OF TEN THOUSAND FRENCH, THAT IN THE FIELD LIE SLAIN; OF PRINCES, IN THIS NUMBER, AND NOBLES BEARING BANNERS, THERE LIE DEAD ONE HUNDRED TWENTY-SIX;
ADDED TO THESE, OF KNIGHTS, ESQUIRES, AND GALLANT GENTLEMEN, EIGHT THOUSAND AND FOUR HUNDRED; OF THE WHICH, FIVE HUNDRED WERE BUT YESTERDAY DUBB'D KNIGHTS;

SO THAT, IN THESE TEN THOUSAND THEY HAVE LOST, THERE ARE BUT SIXTEEN HUNDRED MERCENARIES; THE REST ARE PRINCES, BARONS, LORDS, KNIGHTS, SQUIRES, AND GENTLEMEN OF BLOOD AND QUALITY.
THE NAMES OF THOSE THEIR NOBLES THAT LIE DEAD: CHARLES DELABRETH, HIGH CONSTABLE OF FRANCE; JACQUES OF CHATILLON, ADMIRAL OF FRANCE; THE MASTER OF THE CROSS-BOWS, LORD RAMBURES; GREAT MASTER OF FRANCE, THE BRAVE SIR GUICHARD DAUPHIN,

JOHN DUKE OF ALENÇON, ANTHONY DUKE OF BRABANT, THE BROTHER TO THE DUKE OF BURGUNDY, AND EDWARD DUKE OF BAR; OF LUSTY EARLS, GRANDPRÉ AND ROUSSI, FAUCONBERG AND FOIX, BEAUMONT AND MARLE, VAUDEMONT AND LESTRALE. HERE WAS A ROYAL FELLOWSHIP OF DEATH!
WHERE IS THE NUMBER OF OUR ENGLISH DEAD?

EDWARD THE DUKE OF YORK, THE EARL OF SUFFOLK, SIR RICHARD KETLY, DAVY GAM, ESQUIRE; NONE ELSE OF NAME; AND OF ALL OTHER MEN BUT FIVE AND TWENTY. -- O GOD! THY ARM WAS HERE;
AND NOT TO US, BUT TO THY ARM ALONE, ASCRIBE WE ALL. WHEN, WITHOUT STRATAGEM, BUT IN PLAIN SHOCK AND EVEN PLAY OF BATTLE, WAS EVER KNOWN SO GREAT AND LITTLE LOSS ON ONE PART AND ON THE OTHER? -- TAKE IT, GOD, FOR IT IS NONE BUT THINE!

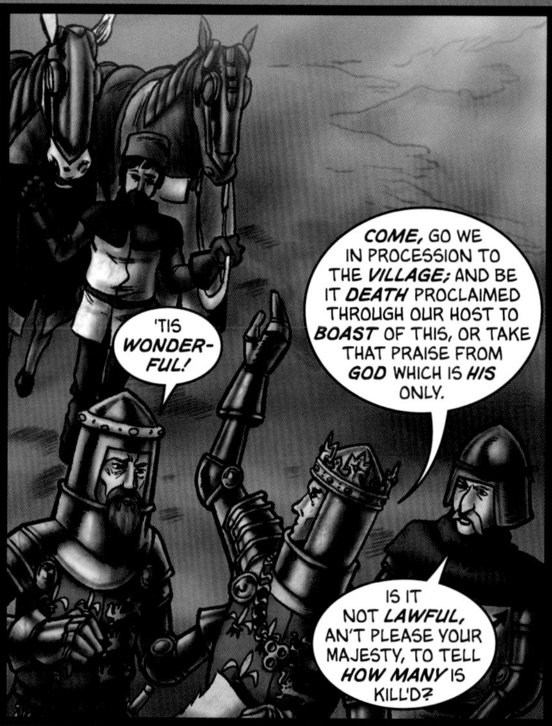
'TIS WONDERFUL!
COME, GO WE IN PROCESSION TO THE VILLAGE; AND BE IT DEATH PROCLAIMED THROUGH OUR HOST TO BOAST OF THIS, OR TAKE THAT PRAISE FROM GOD WHICH IS HIS ONLY.
IS IT NOT LAWFUL, AN'T PLEASE YOUR MAJESTY, TO TELL HOW MANY IS KILL'D?

YES, CAPTAIN; BUT WITH THIS ACKNOWLEDGMENT, THAT GOD FOUGHT FOR US.
YES, MY CONSCIENCE, HE DID US GREAT GOOD.

DO WE ALL HOLY RITES. LET THERE BE SUNG NON NOBIS AND TE DEUM, THE DEAD WITH CHARITY ENCLOS'D IN CLAY, AND THEN TO CALAIS; AND TO ENGLAND THEN, WHERE NE'ER FROM FRANCE ARRIV'D MORE HAPPY MEN.

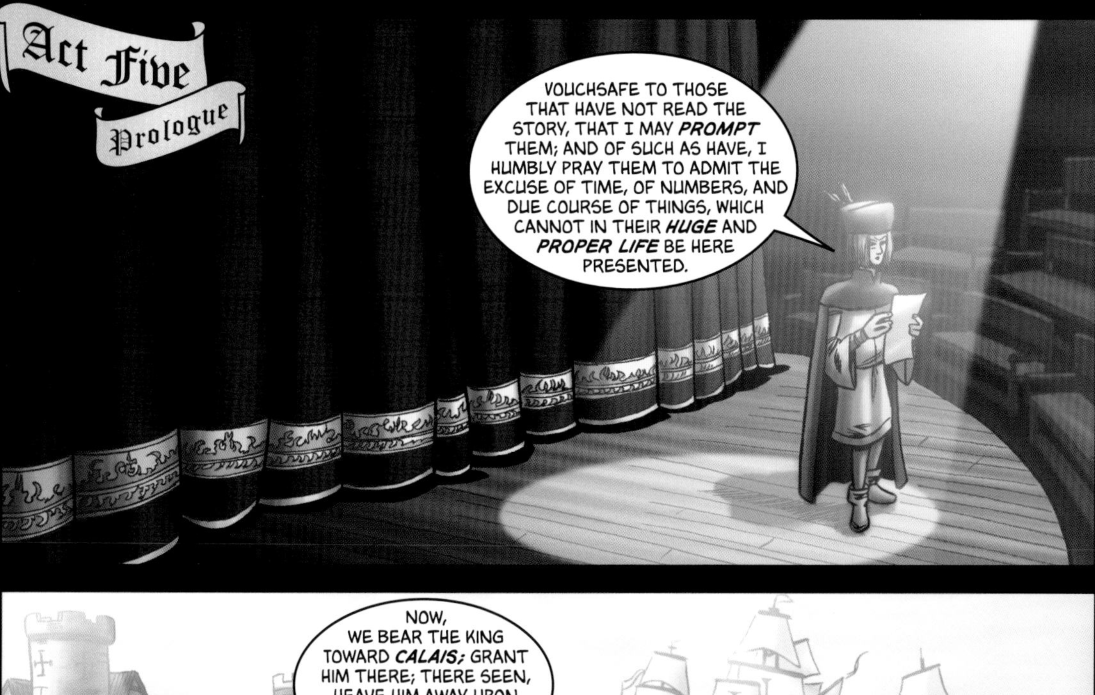
Act Five
Prologue
VOUCHSAFE TO THOSE THAT HAVE NOT READ THE STORY, THAT I MAY PROMPT THEM; AND OF SUCH AS HAVE, I HUMBLY PRAY THEM TO ADMIT THE EXCUSE OF TIME, OF NUMBERS, AND DUE COURSE OF THINGS, WHICH CANNOT IN THEIR HUGE AND PROPER LIFE BE HERE PRESENTED.

NOW, WE BEAR THE KING TOWARD CALAIS; GRANT HIM THERE; THERE SEEN, HEAVE HIM AWAY UPON YOUR WINGED THOUGHTS ATHWART THE SEA.
BEHOLD, THE ENGLISH BEACH PALES IN THE FLOOD WITH MEN, WITH WIVES AND BOYS, WHOSE SHOUTS AND CLAPS OUT-VOICE THE DEEP-MOUTH'D SEA, WHICH LIKE A MIGHTY WHIFFLER 'FORE THE KING SEEMS TO PREPARE HIS WAY.

SO, LET HIM LAND, AND SOLEMNLY SEE HIM SET ON TO LONDON. SO SWIFT A PACE HATH THOUGHT, THAT EVEN NOW YOU MAY IMAGINE HIM UPON BLACKHEATH; WHERE THAT HIS LORDS DESIRE HIM TO HAVE BORNE HIS BRUISED HELMET, AND HIS BENDED SWORD, BEFORE HIM, THROUGH THE CITY. HE FORBIDS IT, BEING FREE FROM VAINNESS AND SELF-GLORIOUS PRIDE; GIVING FULL TROPHY, SIGNAL, AND OSTENT, QUITE FROM HIMSELF, TO GOD.

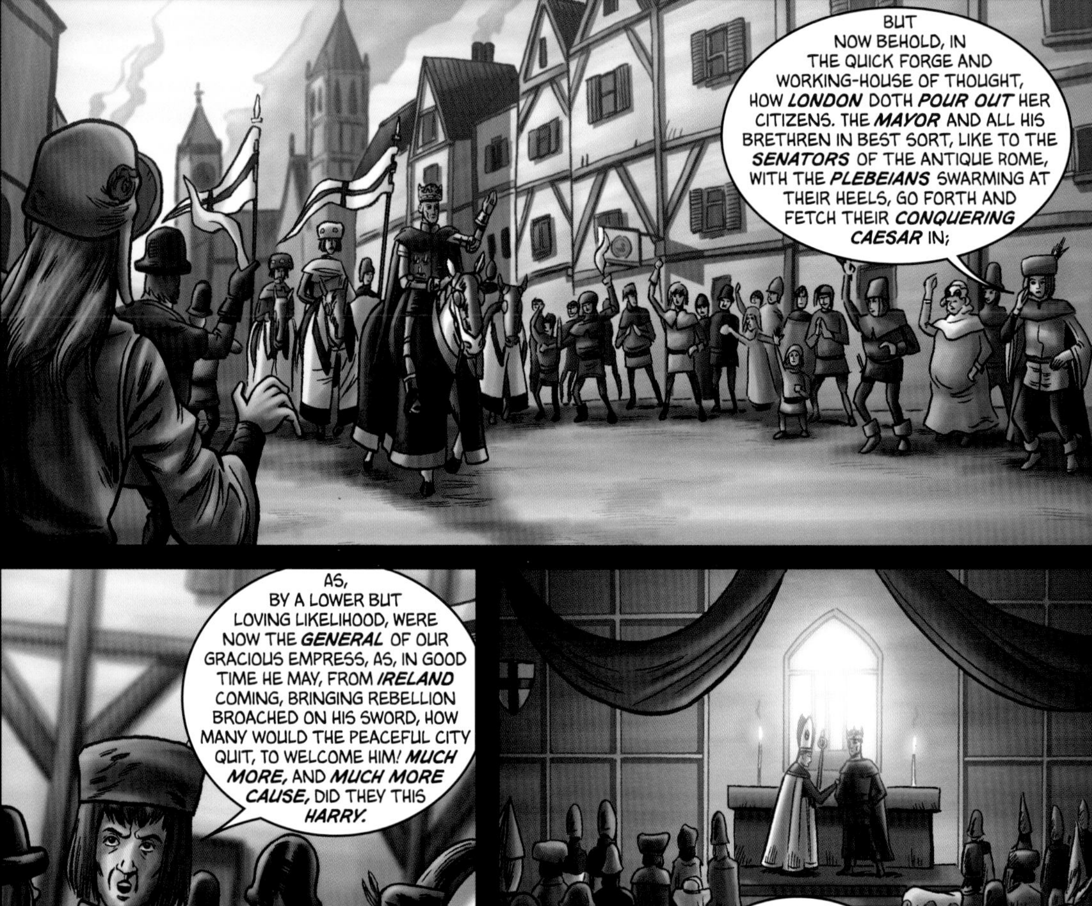
BUT NOW BEHOLD, IN THE QUICK FORGE AND WORKING-HOUSE OF THOUGHT, HOW *LONDON* DOTH *POUR OUT* HER CITIZENS. THE *MAYOR* AND ALL HIS BRETHREN IN BEST SORT, LIKE TO THE *SENATORS* OF THE ANTIQUE ROME, WITH THE *PLEBEIANS* SWARMING AT THEIR HEELS, GO FORTH AND FETCH THEIR *CONQUERING CAESAR* IN;

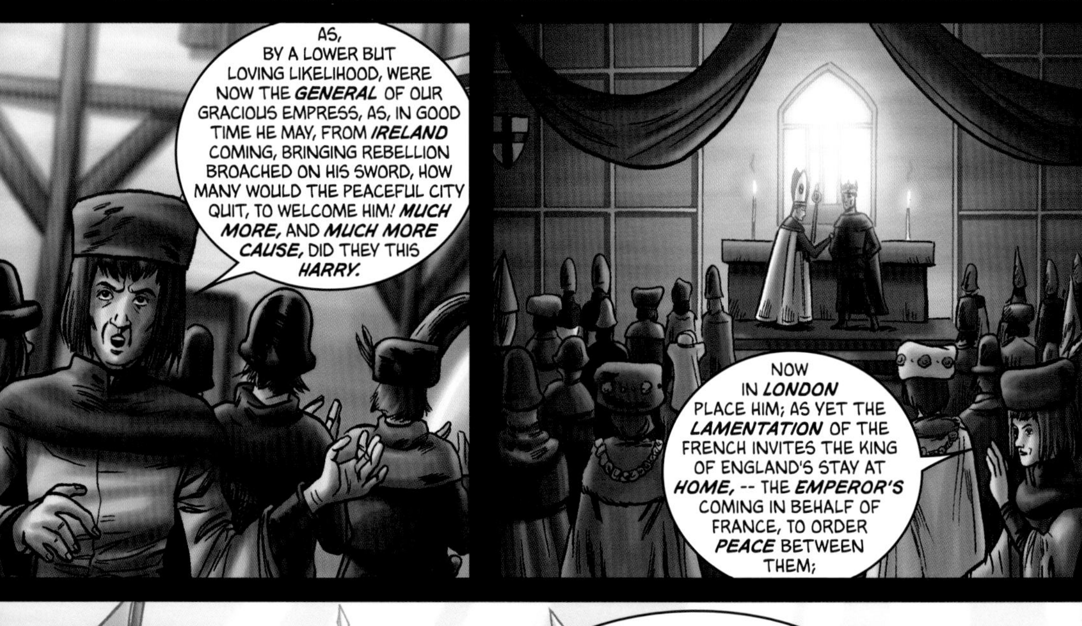
AS, BY A LOWER BUT LOVING LIKELIHOOD, WERE NOW THE *GENERAL* OF OUR GRACIOUS EMPRESS, AS, IN GOOD TIME HE MAY, FROM *IRELAND* COMING, BRINGING REBELLION BROACHED ON HIS SWORD, HOW MANY WOULD THE PEACEFUL CITY QUIT, TO WELCOME HIM! *MUCH MORE,* AND *MUCH MORE CAUSE,* DID THEY THIS *HARRY.*
NOW IN *LONDON* PLACE HIM; AS YET THE *LAMENTATION* OF THE FRENCH INVITES THE KING OF ENGLAND'S STAY AT *HOME,* -- THE *EMPEROR'S* COMING IN BEHALF OF FRANCE, TO ORDER *PEACE* BETWEEN THEM;

AND OMIT ALL THE OCCURRENCES, WHATEVER CHANC'D, TILL HARRY'S *BACK-RETURN* AGAIN TO *FRANCE.* THERE MUST WE BRING HIM; AND MYSELF HAVE PLAY'D THE INTERIM, BY REMEMBERING YOU 'TIS PAST. THEN BROOK ABRIDGMENT, AND YOUR EYES ADVANCE AFTER YOUR THOUGHTS, STRAIGHT BACK AGAIN TO *FRANCE.*

Act Five
Scene One
FRANCE - THE ENGLISH CAMP - THE YEAR IS 1420. FIVE YEARS AFTER ENGLAND'S VICTORY AT AGINCOURT...
NAY, THAT'S RIGHT; BUT WHY WEAR YOU YOUR LEEK TO-DAY? SAINT DAVY'S DAY IS PAST.
THERE IS OCCASIONS AND CAUSES, WHY AND WHEREFORE, IN ALL THINGS. I WILL TELL YOU AS MY FRIEND, CAPTAIN GOWER.

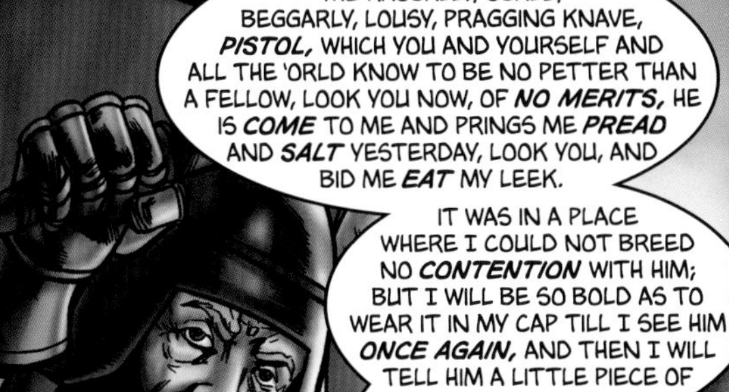
THE RASCALLY, SCALD, BEGGARLY, LOUSY, PRAGGING KNAVE, PISTOL, WHICH YOU AND YOURSELF AND ALL THE 'ORLD KNOW TO BE NO PETTER THAN A FELLOW, LOOK YOU NOW, OF NO MERITS, HE IS COME TO ME AND PRINGS ME PREAD AND SALT YESTERDAY, LOOK YOU, AND BID ME EAT MY LEEK.
IT WAS IN A PLACE WHERE I COULD NOT BREED NO CONTENTION WITH HIM; BUT I WILL BE SO BOLD AS TO WEAR IT IN MY CAP TILL I SEE HIM ONCE AGAIN, AND THEN I WILL TELL HIM A LITTLE PIECE OF MY DESIRES.

WHY, HERE HE COMES, SWELLING LIKE A TURKEY-COCK.
'TIS NO MATTER FOR HIS SWELLINGS NOR HIS TURKEY-COCKS.

GOD PLESS YOU, AUNCHIENT PISTOL! YOU SCURVY, LOUSY KNAVE, GOD PLESS YOU!
HA! ART THOU BEDLAM? DOST THOU THIRST, BASE TROJAN, TO HAVE ME FOLD UP PARCA'S FATAL WEB? HENCE! I AM QUALMISH AT THE SMELL OF LEEK.
I PESEECH YOU HEARTILY, SCURFY, LOUSY KNAVE, AT MY DESIRES, AND MY REQUESTS, AND MY PETITIONS, TO EAT, LOOK YOU, THIS LEEK. BECAUSE, LOOK YOU, YOU DO NOT LOVE IT, NOR YOUR AFFECTIONS AND YOUR APPETITES AND YOUR DIGESTIONS DOES NOT AGREE WITH IT, I WOULD DESIRE YOU TO EAT IT.
NOT FOR CADWALLADER AND ALL HIS GOATS.
THERE IS ONE GOAT FOR YOU.
SMAAAACK!!!
WILL YOU BE SO GOOD, SCALD KNAVE, AS EAT IT?
BASE TROJAN, THOU SHALT DIE.

YOU SAY VERY TRUE, SCALD KNAVE, WHEN GOD'S WILL IS. I WILL DESIRE YOU TO LIVE IN THE MEANTIME, AND EAT YOUR VICTUALS. COME, THERE IS SAUCE FOR IT.

SMAAAACK!!!
YOU CALL'D ME YESTERDAY MOUNTAIN-SQUIRE; BUT I WILL MAKE YOU TO-DAY A SQUIRE OF LOW DEGREE. I PRAY YOU, FALL TO; IF YOU CAN MOCK A LEEK, YOU CAN EAT A LEEK.

ENOUGH, CAPTAIN; YOU HAVE ASTONISH'D HIM.
I SAY, I WILL MAKE HIM EAT SOME PART OF MY LEEK, OR I WILL PEAT HIS PATE FOUR DAYS. -- BITE, I PRAY YOU; IT IS GOOD FOR YOUR GREEN WOUND AND YOUR PLOODY COXCOMB.
MUST I BITE?

YES, CERTAINLY, AND OUT OF DOUBT AND OUT OF QUESTION TOO, AND AMBIGUITIES.
BY THIS LEEK, I WILL MOST HORRIBLY REVENGE.

I EAT AND EAT, I SWEAR--
EAT, I PRAY YOU. WILL YOU HAVE SOME MORE SAUCE TO YOUR LEEK? THERE IS NOT ENOUGH LEEK TO SWEAR BY.

QUIET THY CUDGEL; THOU DOST SEE, I EAT.
MUCH GOOD DO YOU, SCALD KNAVE, HEARTILY. NAY, PRAY YOU, THROW NONE AWAY; THE SKIN IS GOOD FOR YOUR BROKEN COXCOMB. WHEN YOU TAKE OCCASIONS TO SEE LEEKS HEREAFTER, I PRAY YOU, MOCK AT 'EM; THAT IS ALL.

GOOD.
AY, LEEKS *IS* GOOD. -- HOLD YOU, THERE IS A *GROAT* TO HEAL YOUR *PATE.*

ME A GROAT!
YES, VERILY, AND IN TRUTH, YOU SHALL *TAKE* IT; OR I HAVE *ANOTHER* LEEK IN MY POCKET, WHICH YOU SHALL EAT.
I *TAKE* THY GROAT IN EARNEST OF *REVENGE.*

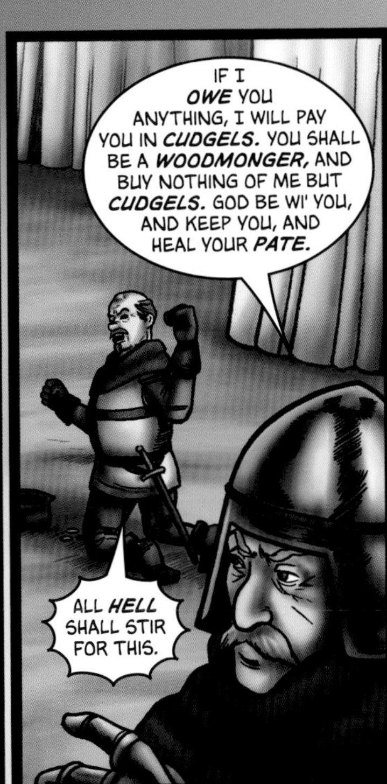
IF I *OWE* YOU ANYTHING, I WILL PAY YOU IN *CUDGELS.* YOU SHALL BE A *WOODMONGER,* AND BUY NOTHING OF ME BUT *CUDGELS.* GOD BE WI' YOU, AND KEEP YOU, AND HEAL YOUR *PATE.*
ALL *HELL* SHALL STIR FOR THIS.

GO, GO; YOU ARE A COUNTERFEIT COWARDLY *KNAVE.*
WILL YOU MOCK AT AN ANCIENT TRADITION, BEGUN UPON AN HONOURABLE RESPECT, AND WORN AS A MEMORABLE TROPHY OF PREDECEASED VALOUR, AND DARE NOT *AVOUCH* IN YOUR DEEDS ANY OF YOUR *WORDS?*

I HAVE SEEN YOU *GLEEKING* AND *GALLING* AT THIS GENTLEMAN TWICE OR THRICE. YOU THOUGHT, BECAUSE HE COULD NOT SPEAK *ENGLISH* IN THE *NATIVE GARB,* HE COULD NOT THEREFORE HANDLE AN ENGLISH *CUDGEL.* YOU FIND IT *OTHERWISE;* AND HENCEFORTH, LET A *WELSH CORRECTION* TEACH YOU A GOOD *ENGLISH CONDITION.*
FARE YE WELL.

DOTH FORTUNE PLAY THE *HUSWIFE* WITH ME NOW? NEWS HAVE I, THAT MY NELL IS *DEAD* I' THE SPITAL OF MALADY OF FRANCE; AND THERE MY RENDEZVOUS IS QUITE CUT OFF. *OLD* I DO WAX; AND FROM MY WEARY LIMBS *HONOUR* IS *CUDGELL'D.*
WELL, *BAWD* I'LL TURN, AND SOMETHING LEAN TO *CUTPURSE* OF QUICK HAND. TO *ENGLAND* WILL I STEAL, AND THERE I'LL *STEAL;* AND *PATCHES* WILL I GET UNTO THESE CUDGELL'D SCARS, AND SWEAR, I GOT THEM IN THE *GALLIA WARS.*

Act Five
Scene Two
FRANCE - THE FRENCH KING'S PALACE. KING HENRY V RETURNS TO MAKE PEACE...
PEACE TO THIS MEETING, WHEREFORE WE ARE MET! UNTO OUR BROTHER FRANCE, AND TO OUR SISTER, HEALTH AND FAIR TIME OF DAY; JOY AND GOOD WISHES TO OUR MOST FAIR AND PRINCELY COUSIN KATHERINE; AND, AS A BRANCH AND MEMBER OF THIS ROYALTY, BY WHOM THIS GREAT ASSEMBLY IS CONTRIV'D, WE DO SALUTE YOU, DUKE OF BURGUNDY; AND, PRINCES FRENCH, AND PEERS, HEALTH TO YOU ALL!
RIGHT JOYOUS ARE WE TO BEHOLD YOUR FACE,MOST WORTHY BROTHER ENGLAND; FAIRLY MET!
SO ARE YOU, PRINCES ENGLISH, EVERY ONE.
SO HAPPY BE THE ISSUE, BROTHER ENGLAND, OF THIS GOOD DAY, AND OF THIS GRACIOUS MEETING, AS WE ARE NOW GLAD TO BEHOLD YOUR EYES;
YOUR EYES, WHICH HITHERTO HAVE BORNE IN THEM AGAINST THE FRENCH, THAT MET THEM IN THEIR BENT, THE FATAL BALLS OF MURDERING BASILISKS.
THE VENOM OF SUCH LOOKS, WE FAIRLY HOPE, HAVE LOST THEIR QUALITY; AND THAT THIS DAY SHALL CHANGE ALL GRIEFS AND QUARRELS INTO LOVE.

TO CRY AMEN TO THAT, THUS WE APPEAR.
YOU ENGLISH PRINCES ALL, I DO SALUTE YOU.
MY DUTY TO YOU BOTH, ON EQUAL LOVE, GREAT KINGS OF FRANCE AND ENGLAND, THAT I HAVE LABOUR'D, WITH ALL MY WITS, MY PAINS, AND STRONG ENDEAVOURS, TO BRING YOUR MOST IMPERIAL MAJESTIES UNTO THIS BAR AND ROYAL INTERVIEW, YOUR MIGHTINESS ON BOTH PARTS BEST CAN WITNESS.
SINCE THEN MY OFFICE HATH SO FAR PREVAIL'D THAT, FACE TO FACE AND ROYAL EYE TO EYE, YOU HAVE CONGREETED, LET IT NOT DISGRACE ME IF I DEMAND, BEFORE THIS ROYAL VIEW, WHAT RUB OR WHAT IMPEDIMENT THERE IS, WHY THAT THE NAKED, POOR, AND MANGLED PEACE, DEAR NURSE OF ARTS, PLENTIES, AND JOYFUL BIRTHS, SHOULD NOT IN THIS BEST GARDEN OF THE WORLD, OUR FERTILE FRANCE, PUT UP HER LOVELY VISAGE?
ALAS! SHE HATH FROM FRANCE TOO LONG BEEN CHAS'D, AND ALL HER HUSBANDRY DOTH LIE ON HEAPS, CORRUPTING IN ITS OWN FERTILITY. HER VINE, THE MERRY CHEERER OF THE HEART, UNPRUNED DIES;
HER HEDGES EVEN-PLEACH'D, LIKE PRISONERS WILDLY OVERGROWN WITH HAIR, PUT FORTH DISORDER'D TWIGS; HER FALLOW LEAS THE DARNEL, HEMLOCK, AND RANK FUMITORY, DOTH ROOT UPON, WHILE THAT THE COULTER RUSTS THAT SHOULD DERACINATE SUCH SAVAGERY;
THE EVEN MEAD, THAT ERST BROUGHT SWEETLY FORTH THE FRECKLED COWSLIP, BURNET, AND GREEN CLOVER, WANTING THE SCYTHE, ALL UNCORRECTED, RANK, CONCEIVES BY IDLENESS, AND NOTHING TEEMS BUT HATEFUL DOCKS, ROUGH THISTLES, KECKSIES, BURS, LOSING BOTH BEAUTY AND UTILITY;
AND AS OUR VINEYARDS, FALLOWS, MEADS, AND HEDGES, DEFECTIVE IN THEIR NATURES, GROW TO WILDNESS. EVEN SO OUR HOUSES, AND OURSELVES, AND CHILDREN, HAVE LOST, OR DO NOT LEARN FOR WANT OF TIME, THE SCIENCES THAT SHOULD BECOME OUR COUNTRY; BUT GROW LIKE SAVAGES, -- AS SOLDIERS WILL, THAT NOTHING DO BUT MEDITATE ON BLOOD, -- TO SWEARING AND STERN LOOKS, DIFFUS'D ATTIRE, AND EVERYTHING THAT SEEMS UNNATURAL.
WHICH TO REDUCE INTO OUR FORMER FAVOUR YOU ARE ASSEMBLED; AND MY SPEECH ENTREATS THAT I MAY KNOW THE LET, WHY GENTLE PEACE SHOULD NOT EXPEL THESE INCONVENIENCES, AND BLESS US WITH HER FORMER QUALITIES.

IF, DUKE OF BURGUNDY, YOU WOULD THE PEACE, WHOSE WANT GIVES GROWTH TO THE IMPERFECTIONS WHICH YOU HAVE CITED, YOU MUST BUY THAT PEACE WITH FULL ACCORD TO ALL OUR JUST DEMANDS; WHOSE TENORS AND PARTICULAR EFFECTS YOU HAVE ENSCHEDUL'D BRIEFLY IN YOUR HANDS.
THE KING HATH HEARD THEM; TO THE WHICH AS YET THERE IS NO ANSWER MADE.
WELL, THEN, THE PEACE, WHICH YOU BEFORE SO URG'D, LIES IN HIS ANSWER.
I HAVE BUT WITH A CURSORARY EYE O'ERGLANC'D THE ARTICLES. PLEASETH YOUR GRACE TO APPOINT SOME OF YOUR COUNCIL PRESENTLY TO SIT WITH US ONCE MORE, WITH BETTER HEED TO RE-SURVEY THEM, WE WILL SUDDENLY PASS OUR ACCEPT AND PEREMPTORY ANSWER.
GO, UNCLE EXETER, AND BROTHER CLARENCE, AND YOU, BROTHER GLOUCESTER, WARWICK, AND HUNTINGTON, GO WITH THE KING; AND TAKE WITH YOU FREE POWER TO RATIFY, AUGMENT, OR ALTER, AS YOUR WISDOMS BEST SHALL SEE ADVANTAGEABLE FOR OUR DIGNITY, ANYTHING IN, OR OUT OF, OUR DEMANDS, AND WE'LL CONSIGN THERETO.
BROTHER, WE SHALL.
WILL YOU, FAIR SISTER, GO WITH THE PRINCES, OR STAY HERE WITH US?
OUR GRACIOUS BROTHER, I WILL GO WITH THEM. HAPLY A WOMAN'S VOICE MAY DO SOME GOOD, WHEN ARTICLES, TOO NICELY URG'D, BE STOOD ON.
YET LEAVE OUR COUSIN KATHERINE HERE WITH US: SHE IS OUR CAPITAL DEMAND, COMPRIS'D WITHIN THE FORE-RANK OF OUR ARTICLES.
SHE HATH GOOD LEAVE.

FAIR KATHERINE, AND MOST FAIR! WILL YOU VOUCHSAFE TO TEACH A SOLDIER TERMS SUCH AS WILL ENTER AT A LADY'S EAR AND PLEAD HIS LOVE-SUIT TO HER GENTLE HEART?
YOUR MAJESTY SHALL MOCK AT ME; I CANNOT SPEAK YOUR ENGLAND.
O FAIR KATHERINE! IF YOU WILL LOVE ME SOUNDLY WITH YOUR FRENCH HEART, I WILL BE GLAD TO HEAR YOU CONFESS IT BROKENLY WITH YOUR ENGLISH TONGUE. DO YOU LIKE ME, KATE?
PARDONNEZ-MOI, I CANNOT TELL VAT IS "LIKE ME."
AN ANGEL IS LIKE YOU, KATE, AND YOU ARE LIKE AN ANGEL.
QUE DIT-IL? QUE JE SUIS SEMBLABLE À LES ANGES?
OUI, VRAIMENT, SAUF VOTRE GRÂCE, AINSI DIT-IL.
I SAID SO, DEAR KATHERINE, AND I MUST NOT BLUSH TO AFFIRM IT.

O BON DIEU! LES LANGUES DES HOMMES SONT PLEINES DE TROMPERIES.

WHAT SAYS SHE, FAIR ONE? THAT THE TONGUES OF MEN ARE FULL OF DECEITS?
OUI, DAT DE TONGUES OF DE MANS IS BE FULL OF DECEITS: DAT IS DE PRINCESS.

THE PRINCESS IS THE BETTER ENGLISHWOMAN. I' FAITH, KATE, MY WOOING IS FIT FOR THY UNDERSTANDING: I AM GLAD THOU CANST SPEAK NO BETTER ENGLISH; FOR IF THOU COULDST, THOU WOULDST FIND ME SUCH A PLAIN KING THAT THOU WOULDST THINK, I HAD SOLD MY FARM TO BUY MY CROWN.
I KNOW NO WAYS TO MINCE IT IN LOVE, BUT DIRECTLY TO SAY, "I LOVE YOU";

THEN, IF YOU URGE ME FARTHER THAN TO SAY, "DO YOU IN FAITH?" I WEAR OUT MY SUIT. GIVE ME YOUR ANSWER; I' FAITH, DO; AND SO CLAP HANDS AND A BARGAIN. HOW SAY YOU, LADY?
SAUF VOTRE HONNEUR, ME UNDERSTAND VELL.
MARRY, IF YOU WOULD PUT ME TO VERSES, OR TO DANCE FOR YOUR SAKE, KATE, WHY YOU UNDID ME; FOR THE ONE, I HAVE NEITHER WORDS NOR MEASURE, AND FOR THE OTHER I HAVE NO STRENGTH IN MEASURE, YET A REASONABLE MEASURE IN STRENGTH.
IF I COULD WIN A LADY AT LEAP-FROG, OR BY VAULTING INTO MY SADDLE WITH MY ARMOUR ON MY BACK, UNDER THE CORRECTION OF BRAGGING BE IT SPOKEN, I SHOULD QUICKLY LEAP INTO A WIFE.
OR IF I MIGHT BUFFET FOR MY LOVE, OR BOUND MY HORSE FOR HER FAVOURS, I COULD LAY ON LIKE A BUTCHER AND SIT LIKE A JACK-AN-APES, NEVER OFF.
BUT, BEFORE GOD, KATE, I CANNOT LOOK GREENLY, NOR GASP OUT MY ELOQUENCE, NOR I HAVE NO CUNNING IN PROTESTATION; ONLY DOWNRIGHT OATHS, WHICH I NEVER USE TILL URGED, NOR NEVER BREAK FOR URGING.
IF THOU CANST LOVE A FELLOW OF THIS TEMPER, KATE, WHOSE FACE IS NOT WORTH SUNBURNING, THAT NEVER LOOKS IN HIS GLASS FOR LOVE OF ANYTHING HE SEES THERE, LET THINE EYE BE THY COOK.
I SPEAK TO THEE PLAIN SOLDIER. IF THOU CANST LOVE ME FOR THIS, TAKE ME; IF NOT, TO SAY TO THEE THAT I SHALL DIE, IS TRUE; BUT FOR THY LOVE, BY THE LORD, NO;

YET I LOVE THEE TOO. AND WHILE THOU LIV'ST, DEAR KATE, TAKE A FELLOW OF PLAIN AND UNCOINED CONSTANCY; FOR HE PERFORCE MUST DO THEE RIGHT, BECAUSE HE HATH NOT THE GIFT TO WOO IN OTHER PLACES; FOR THESE FELLOWS OF INFINITE TONGUE, THAT CAN RHYME THEMSELVES INTO LADIES' FAVOURS, THEY DO ALWAYS REASON THEMSELVES OUT AGAIN.

WHAT! A SPEAKER IS BUT A PRATER: A RHYME IS BUT A BALLAD. A GOOD LEG WILL FALL; A STRAIGHT BACK WILL STOOP; A BLACK BEARD WILL TURN WHITE; A CURLED PATE WILL GROW BALD; A FAIR FACE WILL WITHER; A FULL EYE WILL WAX HOLLOW;
BUT A GOOD HEART, KATE, IS THE SUN AND THE MOON; OR RATHER THE SUN AND NOT THE MOON; FOR IT SHINES BRIGHT AND NEVER CHANGES, BUT KEEPS HIS COURSE TRULY.
IF THOU WOULD HAVE SUCH A ONE, TAKE ME; AND TAKE ME, TAKE A SOLDIER; TAKE A SOLDIER, TAKE A KING. AND WHAT SAY'ST THOU THEN TO MY LOVE? SPEAK, MY FAIR, AND FAIRLY, I PRAY THEE.
IS IT POSSIBLE DAT I SOULD LOVE DE ENEMY OF FRANCE?
NO; IT IS NOT POSSIBLE YOU SHOULD LOVE THE ENEMY OF FRANCE, KATE; BUT, IN LOVING ME, YOU SHOULD LOVE THE FRIEND OF FRANCE;
FOR I LOVE FRANCE SO WELL, THAT I WILL NOT PART WITH A VILLAGE OF IT, I WILL HAVE IT ALL MINE; AND, KATE, WHEN FRANCE IS MINE AND I AM YOURS, THEN YOURS IS FRANCE AND YOU ARE MINE.
I CANNOT TELL VAT IS DAT.
NO, KATE? I WILL TELL THEE IN FRENCH; WHICH I AM SURE WILL HANG UPON MY TONGUE LIKE A NEW-MARRIED WIFE ABOUT HER HUSBAND'S NECK, HARDLY TO BE SHOOK OFF.
JE, QUAND J'AI LE POSSESSION DE FRANCE, ET QUAND VOUS AVEZ LE POSSESSION DE MOI,
LET ME SEE, WHAT THEN? SAINT DENIS BE MY SPEED!
DONC VOTRE EST FRANCE, ET VOUS ÊTES MIENNE.
IT IS AS EASY FOR ME, KATE, TO CONQUER THE KINGDOM, AS TO SPEAK SO MUCH MORE FRENCH. I SHALL NEVER MOVE THEE IN FRENCH, UNLESS IT BE TO LAUGH AT ME.

SAUF VOTRE HONNEUR, LE FRANÇAIS QUE VOUS PARLEZ, IL EST MEILLEUR QUE L'ANGLAIS LEQUEL JE PARLE.
NO, FAITH, IS'T NOT, KATE; BUT THY SPEAKING OF MY TONGUE, AND I THINE, MOST TRULY-FALSELY, MUST NEEDS BE GRANTED TO BE MUCH AT ONE. BUT, KATE, DOST THOU UNDERSTAND THUS MUCH ENGLISH?
CANST THOU LOVE ME?
I CANNOT TELL.
CAN ANY OF YOUR NEIGHBOURS TELL, KATE? I'LL ASK THEM. COME, I KNOW THOU LOVEST ME; AND AT NIGHT, WHEN YOU COME INTO YOUR CLOSET, YOU'LL QUESTION THIS GENTLEWOMAN ABOUT ME;
AND I KNOW, KATE, YOU WILL, TO HER, DISPRAISE THOSE PARTS IN ME THAT YOU LOVE WITH YOUR HEART.

BUT, GOOD KATE, MOCK ME MERCIFULLY; THE RATHER, GENTLE PRINCESS, BECAUSE I LOVE THEE CRUELLY. IF EVER THOU BE'ST MINE, KATE, AS I HAVE A SAVING FAITH WITHIN ME TELLS ME THOU SHALT, I GET THEE WITH SCAMBLING, AND THOU MUST THEREFORE NEEDS PROVE A GOOD SOLDIER-BREEDER.
SHALL NOT THOU AND I, BETWEEN SAINT DENIS AND SAINT GEORGE, COMPOUND A BOY, HALF FRENCH, HALF ENGLISH, THAT SHALL GO TO CONSTANTINOPLE AND TAKE THE TURK BY THE BEARD? SHALL WE NOT? WHAT SAY'ST THOU, MY FAIR FLOWER-DE-LUCE?

I DO NOT KNOW DAT.
NO; 'TIS HEREAFTER TO KNOW, BUT NOW TO PROMISE. DO BUT NOW PROMISE, KATE, YOU WILL ENDEAVOUR FOR YOUR FRENCH PART OF SUCH A BOY; AND FOR MY ENGLISH MOIETY, TAKE THE WORD OF A KING AND A BACHELOR. HOW ANSWER YOU, LA PLUS BELLE KATHERINE DU MONDE, MON TRÈS CHER ET DIVIN DÉESSE?
YOUR MAJESTEE 'AVE FAUSSE FRENCH ENOUGH TO DECEIVE DE MOST SAGE DAMOISELLE DAT IS EN FRANCE.

NOW, FIE UPON MY FALSE FRENCH! BY MINE HONOUR, IN TRUE ENGLISH, I LOVE THEE, KATE; BY WHICH HONOUR I DARE NOT SWEAR THOU LOVEST ME; YET MY BLOOD BEGINS TO FLATTER ME THAT THOU DOST, NOTWITHSTANDING THE POOR AND UNTEMPERING EFFECT OF MY VISAGE.
NOW, BESHREW MY FATHER'S AMBITION! HE WAS THINKING OF CIVIL WARS WHEN
GOT ME; THEREFORE WAS I CREAT
WITH A STUBBORN OUTSIDE, W
AN ASPECT OF IRON, THAT, WHE
I COME TO WOO LADIES, I FRIGHT THEM.
BUT, IN FAITH, KATE, THE ELDER I WAX, THE BETTER I SHALL APPEAR. MY COMFORT IS, THAT OLD AGE, THAT ILL LAYER-UP OF BEAUTY, CAN DO NO MORE SPOIL UPON MY FACE. THOU HAST ME, IF THOU HAST ME, AT THE WORST; AND THOU SHALT WEAR ME, IF THOU WEAR ME, BETTER AND BETTER; AND THEREFORE TELL ME, MOST FAIR KATHERINE, WILL YOU HAVE ME?
PUT OFF YOUR MAIDEN BLUSHES; AVOUCH THE THOUGHTS OF YOUR HEART WITH THE LOOKS OF AN EMPRESS; TAKE ME BY THE HAND, AND SAY, "HARRY OF ENGLAND, I AM THINE";
WHICH WORD THOU SHALT NO SOONER BLESS MINE EAR WITHAL, BUT I WILL TELL THEE ALOUD, "ENGLAND IS THINE, IRELAND IS THINE, FRANCE IS THINE, AND HENRY PLANTAGENET IS THINE"; WHO, THOUGH I SPEAK IT BEFORE HIS FACE, IF HE BE NOT FELLOW WITH THE BEST KING, THOU SHALT FIND THE BEST KING OF GOOD FELLOWS.
COME, YOUR ANSWER IN BROKEN MUSIC; FOR THY VOICE IS MUSIC AND THY ENGLISH BROKEN; THEREFORE, QUEEN OF ALL, KATHERINE, BREAK THY MIND TO ME IN BROKEN ENGLISH.
WILT THOU HAVE ME?
DAT IS AS IT SALL PLEASE DE ROI MON PÈRE.
NAY, IT WILL PLEASE HIM WELL, KATE; IT SHALL PLEASE HIM, KATE.
DEN IT SALL ALSO CONTENT ME.
UPON THAT I KISS YOUR HAND, AND I CALL YOU MY QUEEN.

LAISSEZ, MON SEIGNEUR, LAISSEZ, LAISSEZ! MA FOI, JE NE VEUX POINT QUE VOUS ABAISSEZ VOTRE GRANDEUR EN BAISANT LA MAIN D'UNE DE VOTRE SEIGNEURIE INDIGNE SERVITEUR. EXCUSEZ-MOI, JE VOUS SUPPLIE, MON TRÈS-PUISSANT SEIGNEUR.
THEN I WILL KISS YOUR LIPS, KATE.
LES DAMES ET DEMOISELLES POUR ÊTRE BAISÉES DEVANT LEURS NOCES, IL N'EST PAS LA COUTUME DE FRANCE.
MADAME MY INTERPRETER, WHAT SAYS SHE?
DAT IT IS NOT BE DE FASHION POUR LES LADIES OF FRANCE, -- I CANNOT TELL VAT IS BAISER EN ANGLISH.
TO KISS.
YOUR MAJESTEE ENTENDRE BETTRE QUE MOI.
IT IS NOT A FASHION FOR THE MAIDS IN FRANCE TO KISS BEFORE THEY ARE MARRIED, WOULD SHE SAY?
OUI, VRAIMENT.

O KATE, NICE CUSTOMS CURTSY TO GREAT KINGS. DEAR KATE, YOU AND I CANNOT BE CONFINED WITHIN THE WEAK LIST OF A COUNTRY'S FASHION.
WE ARE THE MAKERS OF MANNERS, KATE; AND THE LIBERTY THAT FOLLOWS OUR PLACES STOPS THE MOUTH OF ALL FIND-FAULTS, AS I WILL DO YOURS, FOR UPHOLDING THE NICE FASHION OF YOUR COUNTRY IN DENYING ME A KISS; THEREFORE, PATIENTLY, AND YIELDING.

YOU HAVE WITCHCRAFT IN YOUR LIPS, KATE; THERE IS MORE ELOQUENCE IN A SUGAR TOUCH OF THEM THAN IN THE TONGUES OF THE FRENCH COUNCIL;
AND THEY SHOULD SOONER PERSUADE HARRY OF ENGLAND THAN A GENERAL PETITION OF MONARCHS.

HERE COMES YOUR FATHER.
GOD SAVE YOUR MAJESTY! MY ROYAL COUSIN, TEACH YOU OUR PRINCESS ENGLISH?
I WOULD HAVE HER LEARN, MY FAIR COUSIN, HOW PERFECTLY I LOVE HER; AND THAT IS GOOD ENGLISH.
IS SHE NOT APT?
OUR TONGUE IS ROUGH, COZ, AND MY CONDITION IS NOT SMOOTH; SO THAT, HAVING NEITHER THE VOICE NOR THE HEART OF FLATTERY ABOUT ME, I CANNOT SO CONJURE UP THE SPIRIT OF LOVE IN HER, THAT HE WILL APPEAR IN HIS TRUE LIKENESS.
PARDON THE FRANKNESS OF MY MIRTH, IF I ANSWER YOU FOR THAT. IF YOU WOULD CONJURE IN HER, YOU MUST MAKE A CIRCLE; IF CONJURE UP LOVE IN HER IN HIS TRUE LIKENESS, HE MUST APPEAR NAKED AND BLIND.
CAN YOU BLAME HER THEN, BEING A MAID YET ROS'D OVER WITH THE VIRGIN CRIMSON OF MODESTY, IF SHE DENY THE APPEARANCE OF A NAKED BLIND BOY IN HER NAKED SEEING SELF? IT WERE, MY LORD, A HARD CONDITION FOR A MAID TO CONSIGN TO.
YET THEY DO WINK AND YIELD, AS LOVE IS BLIND AND ENFORCES.
THEY ARE THEN EXCUS'D, MY LORD, WHEN THEY SEE NOT WHAT THEY DO.
THEN, GOOD MY LORD, TEACH YOUR COUSIN TO CONSENT WINKING.
I WILL WINK ON HER TO CONSENT, MY LORD, IF YOU WILL TEACH HER TO KNOW MY MEANING; FOR MAIDS, WELL SUMMER'D AND WARM KEPT, ARE LIKE FLIES AT BARTHOLOMEW-TIDE, BLIND, THOUGH THEY HAVE THEIR EYES; AND THEN THEY WILL ENDURE HANDLING, WHICH BEFORE WOULD NOT ABIDE LOOKING ON.

THIS MORAL TIES ME OVER TO TIME AND A HOT SUMMER; AND SO I SHALL CATCH THE FLY, YOUR COUSIN, IN THE LATTER END, AND SHE MUST BE BLIND TOO.
AS LOVE IS, MY LORD, BEFORE IT LOVES.
IT IS SO;
AND YOU MAY, SOME OF YOU, THANK LOVE FOR MY BLINDNESS, WHO CANNOT SEE MANY A FAIR FRENCH CITY FOR ONE FAIR FRENCH MAID THAT STANDS IN MY WAY.
YES, MY LORD, YOU SEE THEM PERSPECTIVELY, THE CITIES TURNED INTO A MAID; FOR THEY ARE ALL GIRDLED WITH MAIDEN WALLS THAT WAR HATH NEVER ENTERED.
SHALL KATE BE MY WIFE?
SO PLEASE YOU.
I AM CONTENT, SO THE MAIDEN CITIES YOU TALK OF MAY WAIT ON HER; SO THE MAID THAT STOOD IN THE WAY FOR MY WISH SHALL SHOW ME THE WAY TO MY WILL.
WE HAVE CONSENTED TO ALL TERMS OF REASON.
IS'T SO, MY LORDS OF ENGLAND?
THE KING HATH GRANTED EVERY ARTICLE; HIS DAUGHTER FIRST, AND THEN, IN SEQUEL, ALL, ACCORDING TO THEIR FIRM PROPOSED NATURES.
ONLY, HE HATH NOT YET SUBSCRIBED THIS:
WHERE YOUR MAJESTY DEMANDS, THAT THE KING OF FRANCE, HAVING ANY OCCASION TO WRITE FOR MATTER OF GRANT, SHALL NAME YOUR HIGHNESS IN THIS FORM AND WITH THIS ADDITION,
IN FRENCH, -- NOTRE TRÈS CHER FILS HENRI, ROI D'ANGLETERRE, HÉRITIER DE FRANCE;
AND THUS IN LATIN, -- PRAECLARISSIMUS FILIUS NOSTER HENRICUS, REX ANGLIAE ET HAERES FRANCIAE.

NOR THIS I HAVE NOT, BROTHER, SO DENIED, BUT YOUR REQUEST SHALL MAKE ME LET IT PASS.
I PRAY YOU THEN, IN LOVE AND DEAR ALLIANCE, LET THAT ONE ARTICLE RANK WITH THE REST; AND, THEREUPON, GIVE ME YOUR DAUGHTER.
TAKE HER, FAIR SON, AND FROM HER BLOOD RAISE UP ISSUE TO ME; THAT THE CONTENDING KINGDOMS OF FRANCE AND ENGLAND, WHOSE VERY SHORES LOOK PALE WITH ENVY OF EACH OTHER'S HAPPINESS, MAY CEASE THEIR HATRED;
AND THIS DEAR CONJUNCTION PLANT NEIGHBOURHOOD AND CHRISTIAN-LIKE ACCORD IN THEIR SWEET BOSOMS, THAT NEVER WAR ADVANCE HIS BLEEDING SWORD 'TWIXT ENGLAND AND FAIR FRANCE.

AMEN!
TAN-TARA!
NOW WELCOME, KATE; AND BEAR ME WITNESS ALL, THAT HERE I KISS HER AS MY SOVEREIGN QUEEN.
GOD, THE BEST MAKER OF ALL MARRIAGES, COMBINE YOUR HEARTS IN ONE, YOUR REALMS IN ONE! AS MAN AND WIFE, BEING TWO, ARE ONE IN LOVE, SO BE THERE 'TWIXT YOUR KINGDOMS SUCH A SPOUSAL,
THAT NEVER MAY ILL OFFICE, OR FELL JEALOUSY, WHICH TROUBLES OFT THE BED OF BLESSED MARRIAGE, THRUST IN BETWEEN THE PACTION OF THESE KINGDOMS, TO MAKE DIVORCE OF THEIR INCORPORATE LEAGUE; THAT ENGLISH MAY AS FRENCH, FRENCH ENGLISHMEN, RECEIVE EACH OTHER! GOD SPEAK THIS AMEN!
AMEN!
PREPARE WE FOR OUR MARRIAGE; ON WHICH DAY, MY LORD OF BURGUNDY, WE'LL TAKE YOUR OATH, AND ALL THE PEERS', FOR SURETY OF OUR LEAGUES, THEN SHALL I SWEAR TO KATE, AND YOU TO ME; AND MAY OUR OATHS WELL KEPT AND PROSPEROUS BE!
TAN-TARA!

Epilogue
THUS FAR, WITH ROUGH AND ALL-UNABLE PEN, OUR BENDING AUTHOR HATH PURSU'D THE STORY, IN *LITTLE ROOM* CONFINING *MIGHTY MEN,* MANGLING BY STARTS THE FULL COURSE OF THEIR GLORY.
SMALL TIME, BUT *IN* THAT SMALL MOST *GREATLY* LIV'D THIS STAR OF ENGLAND. *FORTUNE* MADE HIS SWORD, BY WHICH THE WORLD'S BEST GARDEN HE ACHIEV'D, AND OF IT LEFT HIS SON IMPERIAL LORD.

HENRY THE SIXTH, IN INFANT BANDS CROWN'D KING OF FRANCE AND ENGLAND, DID THIS KING SUCCEED; WHOSE STATE SO MANY HAD THE MANAGING, THAT THEY *LOST* FRANCE, AND MADE HIS ENGLAND *BLEED:* WHICH OFT OUR STAGE HATH SHOWN;
AND, FOR THEIR SAKE, IN YOUR FAIR MINDS LET THIS *ACCEPTANCE* TAKE.

End

William Shakespeare

(c.1564 - 1616 AD)

National Portrait Gallery, London

William Shakespeare is one of the most widely read authors and possibly the best dramatist ever to live. The actual date of his birth is not known, but traditionally April 23rd 1564 (St George's Day) has been his accepted birthday, as this was three days before his baptism. He died on the same date in 1616, aged 52.

The life of William Shakespeare can be divided into three acts. The first 20 years of his life were spent in Stratford-upon-Avon where he grew up, went to school, got married and became a father. The next 25 years he spent as an actor and playwright in London; and he spent his last few years back in Stratford-upon-Avon, where he enjoyed his retirement in moderate wealth gained from his successful years in the theatre.

William was the eldest son of tradesman John Shakespeare and Mary Arden, and the third of eight children. His father was later elected mayor of Stratford, which was the highest post a man in civic politics could attain. In sixteenth-century England, William was lucky to survive into adulthood; syphilis, scurvy, smallpox, tuberculosis, typhus and dysentery shortened life expectancy at the time to approximately 35 years. The Bubonic Plague took the lives of many and was believed to have been the cause of death for three of William's seven siblings.

Little is known of William's childhood, other than it is thought that he attended the local grammar school, where he studied Latin and English Literature. In 1582, at the age of 18, William married a local farmer's daughter, Anne Hathaway, who was eight years his senior and three months pregnant. During their marriage they had three children: Susanna, born on May 26th 1583 and twins, Hamnet and Judith, born on February 2nd 1585. Hamnet, William's only son, caught Bubonic Plague and died aged just 11.

Five years into his marriage William moved to London and appeared in many small parts at The Globe Theatre, then one of the biggest theatres in England. His first appearance in public as a poet was in 1593 with "Venus and Adonis" and again in the following year with "The Rape of Lucrece". Later on, in 1599, he became joint proprietor of The Globe.

When Queen Elizabeth died in 1603, she was succeeded by her cousin King James of Scotland. King James supported William and his band of actors and gave them license to call themselves the "King's Men" in return for entertaining the court.

In just 23 years, between approximately 1590 and 1613, William Shakespeare is attributed with writing 38 plays, 154 sonnets and 5 poems. "Love's Labour's Lost" and "The Comedy of

Errors" are thought to be among Shakespeare's earliest plays, followed by, "The Two Gentlemen of Verona" and "Romeo and Juliet". His final play was "Henry VIII", written two years before he died. The cause of his death remains unknown.

He was buried on April 25th 1616, two days after his death, at the Church of the Holy Trinity (the same Church where he had been baptised 52 years earlier). His gravestone bears these words (believed to have been written by William himself):-

"Good friend for Jesus sake forbear,
To dig the dust enclosed here!
Blest be the man that spares these stones,
And curst be he that moves my bones"

At the time of his death, William had substantial properties, which he bestowed on his family and associates from the theatre.

In his will he left his wife, the former Anne Hathaway, his second best bed!

William Shakespeare's last direct descendant died in 1670. She was his granddaughter, Elizabeth.

Henry V, King of England

(c.1387 - 1422 AD)

One of the great warrior kings of medieval England, Henry is most famous for his victory against the French at the Battle of Agincourt.

Henry V, the eldest son of Henry IV and Mary Bohun, was born in 1387. He became Prince of Wales at his father's coronation in 1399. Henry was an accomplished soldier: at 14 he fought the Welsh forces of Owain Glyndwr; in 1403, aged 16, he commanded his father's forces at the battle of Shrewsbury. He was also keen to have a role in government, leading to many disagreements with his father. Henry became king in 1413.

In 1415, he successfully crushed an uprising designed to put Edmund Mortimer, Earl of March, on the throne. Shortly afterwards he sailed for France, which was to be the focus of his attentions for most of his reign. Henry was determined to regain the lands in France previously held by his ancestors and so laid his claim to the French throne. The French war served two purposes - to gain lands lost in previous battles and to focus attention away from any of his cousins' royal ambitions.

He first captured the port of Harfleur and then on October 25th 1415 defeated the French at the Battle of Agincourt. Between 1417 and 1419 Henry followed up this success with the conquest of Normandy. Rouen surrendered in January 1419 and his successes forced the French to agree to the Treaty of Troyes in May 1420.

Henry was recognised as heir to the French throne and married Katherine, the daughter of the French king. In February 1421, Henry returned to England for the first time in three and half years, and he and Katherine undertook a royal progress round the country. In June, he returned to France and died suddenly, probably of dysentery, on August 31st 1422. His nine-month-old son succeeded him (Henry never saw his child). Had Henry lived a mere two months longer, he would have been king of both England and France.

National Portrait Gallery, London

The historian Rafael Holinshed, in the Chronicles of England, summed up Henry's reign as such: "This Henry was a king, of life without spot, a prince whom all men loved, and of none disdained, a captain against whom fortune never frowned, nor mischance once spurned, whose people him so severe a justicer both loved and obeyed (and so humane withal) that he left no offence unpunished, nor friendship unrewarded; a terror to rebels, and suppressor of sedition, his virtues notable, his qualities most praiseworthy."

The Battle of Agincourt October 25th, 1415 (St. Crispin's Day)

'From the thirteenth until the sixteenth century, the national weapon of the English army was the longbow. It was this weapon which conquered Wales and Scotland, gave the English their victories in the Hundred Years War, and permitted England to replace France as the foremost military power in Medieval Europe. The longbow was the machine gun of the Middle Ages: accurate, deadly, possessed of a long-range and rapid rate of fire, the flight of its missiles was liken to a storm. Cheap and simple enough for the yeoman to own and master, it made him superior to a knight on the field of battle.'

The Medieval English Longbow
by Robert E. Kaiser, M.A.

Henry V, King of England, and (according to him and his advisors), parts of France, invaded France on August 13th, 1415 to claim by force his French Kingdom. He first laid siege to the port of Harfleur, in the classic medieval style using primitive cannons (bombards), trenches and ramparts encircling the town's walls. Harfleur finally fell on September 22nd and on October 8th Henry's by now smaller, starving and weary army of some 5,000 archers and 1,000 men-at-arms began a 260-mile march to Calais, hoping to reach England before winter set in.

The main French army started from Rouen in pursuit of the English. On October 24th Henry's scouts spotted the French army near the little river Ternoise, completely blocking the path to Calais. Henry now had no choice but to give battle to the far larger French army of some 15,000-36,000 men (as accurate an estimate as can be given!)

October 25th dawned cold and wet, with the French army drawn up between the villages of Tramecourt on their left flank and Agincourt on their right, forming an impassable blockage on the route to Calais. They were only able to deploy across a narrow front due to the woods that fringed the two villages.

The English army was gathered in between the woods at the other end of the field, roughly a kilometre from the French.

This meant that the battle took place on recently ploughed fields between the woods - a decisive factor in the final outcome.

The French formed three massive divisions (called battles), with the first two consisting of dismounted men-at-arms with cavalry on their flanks, and a third division consisting entirely of cavalry. Crossbowmen and archers were to take up position at the front of the divisions.

The French planned to shower the English with arrows, then move in with the flanking cavalry to take out the bowmen of the English army, as the French men-at-arms moved in to dispatch the English infantry.

By 11am the English could wait no longer for a French advance. Henry's troops were tired and weak from hunger, dysentery and the long, wet march; so they advanced to within 200 metres of the French troops. At this point the English archers halted and pounded in pointed wooden stakes (palings) in front of their positions to keep the French cavalry at bay.

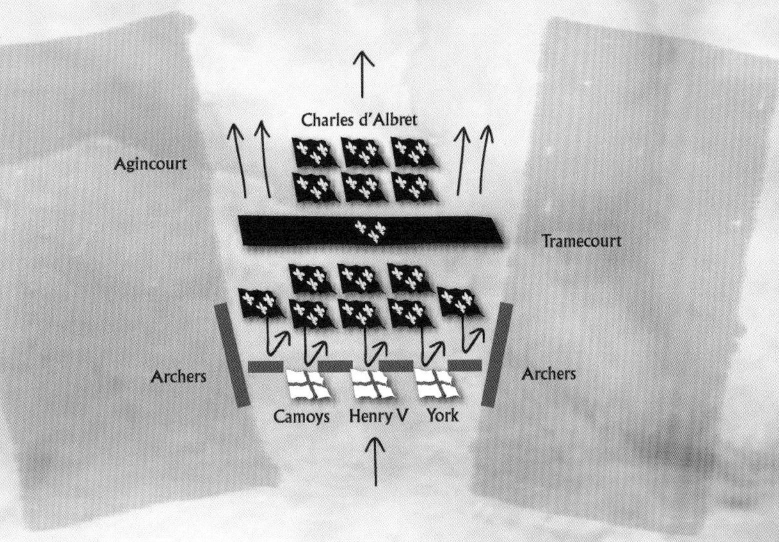

The English advance threw the French into confusion and precipitated the premature charge of the French heavy cavalry. The cavalry advanced slowly in the mud and under a hail of arrows. They tried to outflank the English but were hemmed in by the woods and forced to continue with a frontal assault. They quickly found themselves and their horses impaled upon the stakes and under unremitting fire from the English archers. The English line held and what was left of the French cavalry was forced to withdraw.

The first French division of men-at-arms lumbered forward after the failure of the cavalry assault. The English arrows took their toll but the French finally closed with the English men-at-arms. Many French nobles had already been killed by arrows and, as the line pushed forward, many more men fell and were trampled to death, hampered by their heavy armour.

Initially the impact of the French advance drove the English line back, but they quickly recovered; and the English men-at-arms and archers joined the fray with mallets, axes and swords, easily dispatching the tightly packed and heavily armoured columns of French knights. As the first French division was being decimated, the remaining English archers kept up a heavy hail of arrows on the advancing second French division of men-at-arms. The knights in this second division saw what was happening to their comrades and began leaving the field without engaging the English. This left the mounted French third division as the last hope for the French to snatch a victory from defeat. However, attacking the English longbowmen was more than those troops wished to contemplate and they too began drifting away through the Tramecourt Woods.

The English interpreted this movement as a potential threat, with the French moving through the woods and possibly threatening the English rear. This news, coupled with reports that the English baggage train had been attacked, led Henry to order the deaths of all the prisoners, as there were not enough soldiers left to guard the prisoners and fend off another attack.

Many prisoners were killed but some English knights who were horrified by this order saved their prisoners. It is believed that more French deaths took place during this slaughter, than during the battle itself.

By the end of the day it is estimated that between 7,000 and 10,000 French had perished but only 500 English. Henry and his army went on to Calais and then back to England, with a number of French nobles held to ransom.

It was an incredible English victory that would go down in the annals of warfare.

Arguably, the deciding factor for the outcome was the terrain. The narrow field of battle, of recently ploughed land hemmed in by dense woodland, favoured the English.

However, Shakespeare appears to have favoured a rather different rationale, basing the victory on the will of God, given that Henry's cause was just.

Page Creation

In order to create three versions of the same book, the play is first adapted into three scripts: Original Text, Plain Text and Quick Text. While the degree of complexity changes for each script, the artwork remains the same for all three books.

Above is a rough thumbnail sketch of pages 86 and 87 created from the script. Once the rough sketch is approved it is redrawn as a clean finished pencil sketch (left).

318. Henry kneels inside his tent. He joins his hands in prayer.

	QUICK TEXT	PLAIN ENGLISH TEXT	ORIGINAL TEXT
HENRY (TH)	And don't let the way my father took the crown from Richard II go against me now. I've re-buried Richard's body in Westminster Abbey. I've cried with regret and I've given 500 pensions to the holy poor to pray for my father's pardon.	Not today, Oh Lord. Don't think today about my father's fault in taking the crown! I've re-buried Richard II's body in Westminster Abbey and I've cried more remorseful tears on it than the drops of blood it spilled. I've given pensions to 500 paupers to pray twice daily to heaven for my father's pardon…	Not to–day, O Lord! O! not to–day, think not upon the fault My father made in compassing the crown. I Richard's body have interred new, And on it have bestow'd more contrite tears Than from it issued forced drops of blood. Five hundred poor I have in yearly pay, Who twice a day their wither'd hands hold up Toward heaven, to pardon blood;

319. The Duke of Gloucester (Henry's brother) enters the tent and watches the King in prayer.

HENRY (TH)	I've built two chapels where priests sing and pray for Richard's soul. And I'll do more. I'll do more, even if it's all for nothing…	…and I've built two chapels where devout priests sing and pray for Richard's soul. I'll do even more, even if everything I do means nothing, since it's all just a plea for personal pardon.	and I have built Two chantries, where the sad and solemn priests Sing still for Richard's soul. More will I do; Though all that I can do is nothing worth, Since that my penitence comes after all, Imploring pardon.
GLOUCESTER	My lord!	My liege!	My liege!

320. Henry doesn't look up.

HENRY	That's my brother Gloucester's voice. I know what you want. I'll go with you, because everything waits for me.	My brother Gloucester's voice? Yes, I know what you want. I'll go with you. The day, my friends, and all other things wait for me.	My brother Gloucester's voice? —Ay; I know thy errand, I will go with thee: — The day, my friends, and all things stay for me.

From the pencil sketch we can now create an inked version of the same page (below).

Inking is not simply tracing over the pencil sketch, it is the process of using black ink to fill in the shaded areas and to add clarity and cohesion to the "pencils".

The "inks" give us the final outline and the next stage is to add colour to the inked image.

Adding colour brings the page and its characters to life.

Each character has a detailed Character Study drawn. This is useful for the inkers and the colourists to refer to and ensures continuity throughout the book.

The last stage of page creation is to add the speech and any sound effects.

Speech bubbles are created from the script and are laid over the finished coloured pages.

Three versions of lettered pages are produced for the three different versions of Henry V. These are then saved as final artwork pages and compiled into books.

Original Text

MY BROTHER GLOUCESTER'S VOICE?
AY; I KNOW THY ERRAND, I WILL GO WITH THEE:
THE DAY, MY FRIENDS, AND ALL THINGS STAY FOR ME.

Shakespeare Around the Globe

The Globe Theatre and Shakespeare

Although it's hard to appreciate today, theatres were actually a new idea in William Shakespeare's time. The very first theatre in Elizabethan London to only show plays, aptly called 'The Theatre', was introduced by an entrepreneur called James Burbage. In fact, 'The Globe Theatre', possibly the most famous theatre of that era, was built from the timbers of 'The Theatre'. The landlord of 'The Theatre' was Giles Allen, who was a Puritan that disapproved of theatrical entertainment. When he decided to enforce a huge rent increase in the winter of 1598, the theatre members dismantled the building piece by piece and shipped it across the Thames to Southwark for reassembly. Allen was powerless to do anything, as the company owned the wood (although he spent three years in court trying to sue the perpetrators)!

The report of the dismantling party (written by Schoenbaum) says: *"ryotous... armed... with divers and manye unlawfull and offensive weapons... in verye ryotous outragious and forcyble manner and contrarye to the lawes of your highnes Realme... and there pulling breaking and throwing downe the sayd Theater in verye outragious violent and riotous sort to the great disturbance and terrefyeing not onlye of your subjectes... but of divers others of your majesties loving subjectes there neere inhabitinge."*

William Shakespeare became a part owner of this new Globe Theatre in 1599. It was one of four major theatres in the area, along with the Swan, the Rose, and the Hope. The exact physical structure of the Globe is unknown, although scholars are fairly sure of some details through drawings from the period. The theatre itself was a closed structure with an open courtyard where the stage stood. Tiered galleries around the open area accommodated the wealthier patrons who could afford seats, and those of the lower classes - the 'groundlings' - stood around the platform or 'thrust' stage during the performance of a play. The space under and behind the stage was used for special effects, storage and costume changes. Surprisingly, although the entire structure was not very big by modern standards, it is known to have accommodated fairly large crowds - as many as 3,000 people - during a single performance.

The Globe II

In 1613, the original Globe Theatre burned to the ground when a cannon shot during a performance of "Henry VIII" set fire to the thatched roof of the gallery. Undeterred, the company completed a new Globe (this time with a tiled roof) on the foundations of its predecessor. Opened in 1614, Shakespeare didn't write any new plays for this theatre. He retired to Stratford-Upon-Avon that year, and died two years later. Despite that, performances continued until 1642, when the Puritans closed down all theatres and places of entertainment. Two years later, the Puritans razed the building to the ground in order to build tenements upon the site. No more was to be seen of the Globe for 352 years.

Shakespeare's Globe

Led by the vision of the late Sam Wanamaker, work began on the construction of a new Globe in 1993, close to the site of the original theatre. It was completed three years later, and Queen Elizabeth II officially opened the New Globe Theatre on June 12th, 1997 with a production of "Henry V".

The New Globe Theatre is as faithful a reproduction as possible to the Elizabethan theatre, given that the details of the original are only known from sketches of the time. The building can accommodate 1,500 people between the galleries and the 'groundlings.'

www.shakespeares-globe.org

There are also replica Globe theatres in Rome and Berlin, The Old Globe in San Diego, and even an 'Ice Globe' in Sweden. In New York, ambitious plans are underway to convert a decaying military fortification, built to defend America against the British in the War of 1812, into a New Globe – and amazingly, the existing structure has an identical footprint to Shakespeare's Globe Theatre in London.

Foster and Partners

New York: **www.newglobe.org**
Rome: **www.globetheatreroma.com**
San Diego: **www.oldglobe.org**
Berlin: **www.shakespeare-company.de**
Sweden: **www.athropolis.com**

Shakespeare Today

Our fascination with William Shakespeare has not diminished over the centuries. Despite being written over 400 years ago, his plays are still read in schools, adapted into graphic novels(!), made into films, performed in theatres the world over, and are still taken to the public by acting troupes, such as the **British Shakespeare Company**. The tradition of open-air theatre is deeply rooted in British culture. For over a thousand years companies have created theatres in the centre of towns, erecting a pageant wagon or scaffolding stage from which to perform great historical and classical drama for a mass audience. These open-air acting troupes, which weathered the theatrical shifts from medieval Mystery and Morality plays towards the sophisticated characterisation of Elizabethan drama, were the inspiration behind the British Shakespeare Company. The pageant wagons, and later inn-yards and amphitheatres outside London, were for centuries the only means by which Shakespeare and others could communicate with audiences beyond the capital. Today, more than 100,000 people watch BSC performances each year. With a full company of players and performances that feature original live music and songs, beautiful period costumes and the magic of a summer's evening, the BSC is fulfilling that primary aim of all performers throughout the years: to enchant and delight audiences of all classes and ages. **www.britishshakespearecompany.com**

On the other side of the Atlantic, New York has **Shakespeare in the Park**. Since 1962, The Public Theater has staged productions of Shakespeare at The Delacorte Theater in Central Park. These performances are seen by approximately 80,000 New Yorkers and visitors each summer. In fact, since its inception, many of today's most acclaimed actors have taken part, including Morgan Freeman, Meryl Streep, Denzel Washington, Christopher Walken, Kevin Kline, Natalie Portman, Marcia Gay Harden, Philip Seymour Hoffman, Patrick Stewart, Jeff Goldblum and Billy Crudup, as well as dozens of directors and designers. **www.publictheater.org**

Another groundbreaking scheme belongs to the **Canadian Adaptations of Shakespeare Project**. CASP aims to be the largest collection of teaching and learning resources related to Shakespeare on the Internet. They are continuing to develop resources that use adaptation theory to study and teach about Shakespeare's works and their cultural effects, drawing on multimedia presentations and even including an arcade-style game to promote learning.

www.canadianshakespeares.ca

It seems that whatever time brings to our global society, and whatever developments take place within our cultures, William Shakespeare continues to have a place in our hearts and in our lives.